WORD MAGIC

"A charming bit of whimsy about a French waif and some exceedingly human puppets. As a matter of fact, Mr. Gallico's seven dolls have a lot more life in them than many purportedly flesh-and-blood characters who have creaked through recent fiction."

— Martin Levin
Saturday Review
December 4, 1954

"It is difficult to describe and impossible to pinpoint the tenuous, even nebulous word magic that successfully carries a reader into the world of fantasy and make-believe. It is perhaps best delineated as a quality, a kind of fragile atmosphere that, once established cannot be broken. Mr. Gallico creates this atmosphere when he writes the sequences with Mouche and the puppets."

— Andrea Parke
The New York Times Book Review
November 28, 1954

PAUL GALLICO

LOVE OF SEVEN DOLLS

ILLUSTRATIONS BY QUAY

**INTERNATIONAL POLYGONICS, LTD.
NEW YORK CITY**

LOVE OF SEVEN DOLLS

Cover and illustrations: Copyright © 1989 by International
Polygonics, Ltd.
Library of Congress Card Catalog No. 89-80435
ISBN 1-55882-013-2

Printed and manufactured in the United States of America.
First IPL printing July 1989.
10 9 8 7 6 5 4 3 2 1

TO BURR TILLSTROM AND FRAN ALLISON

Part One

In Paris, in the spring of our times, a young girl was about to throw herself into the Seine.

She was a thin, awkward creature with a wide mouth and

short black hair. Her body was all bones and hollows where there should have been curves and flesh. Her face was appealing, but it was now gaunt with hunger and the misery of failure. Her eyes were haunting, large, liquid, dark, and filled with despair.

Her name was Marelle Guizec, but her nickname was Mouche. She was an orphan, a Bretonnaise from the village of Plouha, near St. Brieuc. Wretched though she was, some of the mystery of this mysterious land still clung to her. It manifested itself in the grace with which she walked, as though still clad in the swinging peasant skirts, the gravity of her glance, her innocence and primitive mind, in which for all her youth—she was only twenty-two—were dark corners of Celtic brooding. One of these was now leading her to her death.

She wished to die, for like many young girls from the provinces she had come to Paris to try to succeed in the theater. She had failed most miserably. There was truly no single soul in the world who cared what became of her now that she had been dismissed from the lowly *Moulin Bleu Revue* as incompetent and incapable of inspiring interest or desire among the patrons. There was no one who was her friend. The paltry francs she would receive would feed and shelter her for only a few days. After that she must starve or sell herself.

Do you remember Paris that May when spring came early and the giant candelabra of the chestnut trees in bloom illuminated the beautiful city?

The sun-washed days were warm, but the nights still cold and often windy. By day Paris played at summer; the children appeared with their nurses by the Rond Point, the scent of perfumed women lingered on the boulevards, the gay shops glittered in the sunlight; the sky was a canopy of that particular blue that seems to exist only over France. But in the evening the chill drove people off the streets.

It was for this reason that the early season street carnival beyond the Pont de Neuilly was preparing to pack up and depart in disappointment, for it had expected to do most of its business after dark.

Its chain of nakedly glaring electric light bulbs and smoking gasoline flares stretched along one side of the Avenue du Général de Gaulle from the Rond Point de la Défense all the way to the bridge across the Seine that gave entrance to Paris from the west.

The clangor of the street fair, the carrousel music, the cries of the barkers and snapping of rifles in the shooting galleries, the ringing of bells and snorting of the engines that operated the rides had given way to the more prosaic sounds of dismantling, hammering, and sawing, and the noise of boards and metal sheets being thrown to the ground and flats being loaded on trucks was drowning out the last of the mechanical music makers.

Only a few hardy stragglers defied the chill breeze and hung about as swings, whip rides, auto dodgems, stages, and tents began to come down. By morning, nothing but the litter in the street and the worn patches on the earth at the side of the broad avenue would indicate where the fair had been.

In the drafty outdoor canvas-enclosed square that served the shivering girls of the tawdry *Moulin Bleu Revue* as a dressing room, Mouche, having surrendered the scanty bits of costume that had been lent her, donned her clothes and reflected for the last time upon the collapse of her hopes.

The cheap grind-and-strip show was packing to move on to St. Germain, but she had not been good enough even to keep this job and go along. At the conclusion of the final performance that night, the manager had discharged her, saying, "Too thin, too thin, my child. Our girls run more to meat and juice. I heard someone in the audience say of you, 'Here comes that little plucked chicken again.' Sorry, but you won't do. If a girl cannot sing or dance, at least she must look like something."

It was true. Mouche excited pity rather than desire.

Her story was the usual one of the stage-struck girl encouraged by perhaps a local success at some amateur theatricals. Orphaned during the war, she had lived with a great-aunt who had likewise died when she was but sixteen. She had then gone to St. Brieuc and secured a job cleaning the Town Hall, saving her money until she had sufficient to make the journey to Paris.

And there she had come face to face with the fact that she had neither the talent nor the physical equipment to further her ambitions.

She had been pawed by dirty men and stripped by agents and managers who had examined the merchandise of her body and in the end had laughed and turned her out undamaged, for her innocence and chastity were an affront to their consciences and they wished to have her out of their sight.

Occasionally she had succeeded in securing a trial in the cabarets of Pigalle and Montmartre and this had kept her from starvation, but she never was able to hold a job and, descending always lower, had ended with the strip revue in the street fair and now had been judged unfit for this most miserable of forms of entertainment. Not even to the tawdry audiences that filed through the tents for a few francs could her body deliver a single, solitary illusion.

It was this that determined her to do away with herself, for the dismissal pointed up the fact that even had she come to the point of selling herself to keep from starvation she would have found no buyers.

Mouche looked about her once more at the chattering girls who at least were useful in that they could walk across a plank stage and make men shout or laugh and whistle. Then she collected her few belongings and packed them into the small straw valise she had brought with her, as she had expected to be traveling with them in the bus to their next stop.

She would have no further need for these articles, but she could not bring herself to abandon them. The straw suitcase would be found standing on the parapet of the Pont de Neuilly in the morning when the police came with their long poles and fished her body out of the Seine.

She picked up the bag and without a backward glance went out of the enclosure. It seemed as if in anticipation of her rendezvous the light was already extinguished from her eyes. Her thin shoulders had the droop of the beaten girl so easily recognized in France, the soon-to-be suicide. . . .

The manager emerged just then and, recognizing it, was for a moment moved to pity and tempted to reverse his decision and call her back. But he hesitated. If one had pity on every little scarecrow from the provinces, where would one end?

And yet there was something appealing about the little one. He had felt it. Not what the customers wanted, but still—if one could catch what it was . . . By the time he had decided to yield to his better nature and called after her, "Allo! Mouche! Wait. Come back. Perhaps . . ." she was gone.

Mouche, marching unseeing, like one already dead, toward the Seine, thought briefly of her childhood in Brittany and saw again the blue-green seas crashing in white foam onto the black rocks, the sunny fields cut by crooked stone walls, and the flames of the poppies from the midst of which rose the ancient stone crosses and still more ancient Druid menhirs.

The fisher boats beat their way home; children played in the sand; the postman on his bicycle rode by; women stopped for a gossip outside the baker's cottage, and for a moment Mouche smelled the fresh bread and crisp rolls. She was in church again and heard the rustle of starched headdresses and the sigh of the organ. Snatches of melodies of old songs drifted through her mind and for an instant she saw her mother's work-worn hands arranging her First Communion dress. Recollections came to her of old friends, a gray rabbit she had once owned and a tortoise, a yellow cat and a duck that had only one leg. She remembered the eyes of wild things that sometimes peered from the depth of hedges in not unfriendly fashion.

Looking into this bright garden of life as through a door opened in a wall, she could not see how much there was to live for, that she was young and that one could build anew upon the ashes of failure. The black, smoky night, so noisy, cold, and hostile, encouraged only the sunless corners of her mind. She hurried forward as one who goes unseeing.

Something or someone cried out of the darkness: "Hello there, you with the suitcase! Where are you going and what's your hurry?"

Mouche paused, startled and bewildered, for the shrill little voice obviously was directed at her, but she could not make out whence it came. The impudence of the query angered her, for it had the effect of returning her to a world she had in effect already departed.

The next words, reaching her out of the darkness, startled her even more.

"It's cold at the bottom of the river, little one, and the eels and the crayfish eat your flesh."

This was magic, and Mouche had all the superstition and belief in the supernatural of the Bretonnaise. Fearfully she gazed about her for the source of the voice that could guess her secret.

By the wavering light of a gasoline flare she saw only an empty puppet booth with an oilcloth sign across the top announcing: "CAPITAINE COQ ET SA FAMILLE." Nearby on one side a dirty-looking gypsy fortuneteller was quarreling with her husband over the small pickings while they occupied themselves with dismantling their tent. On the other, two men were engaged in loading a strength-testing machine onto a small truck. No one appeared to be aware of the presence of the girl.

The insistent piping voice attacked her again: "What's the big tragedy? Your boy friend give you the air? There's plenty more fish in the sea."

Peering through the smoky haze, Mouche now saw that the puppet booth was not entirely deserted, as she had first thought. A doll was perched on the counter, or at any rate, half a doll, for no legs were visible, a boy with red hair, bulb nose, and pointed ears. He was regarding her with impertinent painted eyes and a curiously troubled expression on his countenance. In the shifting yellow flicker of the gasoline flare he seemed to be beckoning to her.

"Well?" he said. "Cat got your tongue? Speak up when you're spoken to."

In her first alarm Mouche had set down her valise. Now she picked it up and walked with it slowly closer to the booth to examine this astonishing little creature.

Still feeling strangely indignant at being thus unceremoniously accosted, she heard herself to her surprise reply: "Really, what makes you think it is any of your concern?"

The puppet looked her carefully up and down. "Oh," he said, "out of a job, down at the heels, and huffy too. I was only trying to be polite and pass the time."

"By speaking to strangers to whom you have not been introduced?" Mouche chided. "And getting personal too. How would you like it if I . . . ?" She paused, realizing for the first time that she was addressing the little creature as though it were a human being. And yet it was not really strange that she should, for its attitudes and movements were so real and even the expression on the painted face seemed to change with the angle of the head.

"Oh, I wouldn't mind," he concluded for her. "Everyone likes to talk about themselves. Would you care to hear my life story? I was born in a tree on Christmas Eve . . ."

There was a swift movement, and a girl puppet appeared on the counter. She had golden ringlets, wide, staring eyes, and a small, discontented mouth.

She turned this way and that, appearing to inspect Mouche from all angles. Then she said, "My goodness, Carrot Top, where do you find them?"

The leprechaun puppet took a bow and said, "Not bad, eh?"

The girl gave a little shriek. "My goodness, Carrots, you surely don't think she's pretty. . . . Why, she's nothing but skin and bones."

Carrot Top, with a twist of his head, managed to look reflective. "Well, I'll admit her legs aren't much to look at, Gigi, but she has nice eyes and there's something about her that . . ."

"Country trash, if you ask me, and probably no better than she should be," Gigi murmured, and, folding her hands piously, gazed skyward.

"Yes," Carrot Top agreed, "a country cousin all right. But still, you know . . ."

Mouche felt that it was enough. She stamped her foot at the

mocking little creatures and cried, "Really! How dare you two stand there and discuss me—— Don't you know that is the worst manners?"

Carrot Top seemed taken aback and looked worried. He replied, "Dear me. Perhaps you are right. We've all been running somewhat wild of late. Maybe what we need is a little discipline. Why don't you try saying something rude to us?"

Gigi flounced petulantly. "Well, I for one don't intend to remain here to be abused by a scarecrow," and vanished beneath the counter.

Carrot Top looked after her and shook his head slowly. "She's not getting any better-tempered. Well, go ahead. I don't mind being insulted."

Mouche could not repress a smile. "I can't. I think I like you."

"Oh! Do you really?" Carrot Top contrived to look both pleased and startled. "That wants some thinking over. I'll see you later maybe."

He vanished likewise but was immediately replaced by the fore part of a red fox with a long, pointed nose and a sardonic grin. There was a leer in his avid eyes and a worse one in his voice. For a moment he watched the girl warily, then, appearing to smile a sly, oily smile, rasped at Mouche, "Hello, baby!"

Mouche gave him a severe look. "Don't you hello me," she

admonished. "You're a wicked scoundrel if ever I saw one."

The fox turned his head on his neck so that he looked hurt. "I am not. I can't help my looks. Come on over here and see. Put your hand out."

Mouche moved closer to the booth and extended her hand gingerly. The expression on the pale brow beneath her cheap little hat was half worried, yet she felt herself charmed. The fox gently snuggled his chin onto Mouche's palm and heaved a deep sigh. "There," he said, "you see how you've misjudged me?" He cocked an eye up at her.

Mouche was not to be deceived. She remarked, "I'm not sure I have at all."

"Heart like a kitten," the fox insisted, snuggling his chin deeper into the cup of Mouche's palm, and then added, "The trouble is, nobody trusts me. You would trust me, wouldn't you?"

She was about to reply that she wouldn't dream of doing so, when he moved his head and looked up at her once more. His mouth opened and closed silently. Surely it was the smoky light and the dancing shadows, but Mouche thought she saw such an expression of yearning, such a desire for trust on the sharp, clever face that she felt herself unaccountably touched and cried from her own heart, "Oh yes. I would. . . ."

She had all but forgotten whither she had been bound, or why.

Nor did it strike her as at all strange that she should be standing there by the counter of a puppet booth conversing with a scallywag of a fox. Where she came from, one talked not only with the little animals of the fields and the birds in the trees, but the trees themselves and the running brooks, and often one whispered one's innermost secrets or heart's desire to one of the gray dolmens that stood so mysteriously in a meadow.

The fox sighed again. "I knew I'd find someone innocent enough someday. What's your name, baby?"

"Marelle. But they call me Petite Mouche."

"Little fly, eh? My name is Mr. Reynardo, J. L. Reynardo— Rey to my friends. Where are you from?"

"Plouha, near St. Brieuc."

The fox suddenly raised his head so that he was looking at her sidelong out of one wicked eye. He quoted from an old proverb, "Beware a sleeping dog, a praying drunk, or a Bretonnaise."

Mouche snatched her hand away and quoted back at him: "When the fox preaches, guard your geese. . . ."

Mr. Reynardo let out a yapping bark of laughter and retired to the side of the booth. "Kid, you've got some spunk in that skinny carcass of yours. Hasn't she, friends?"

This last was addressed to the workmen, who had finished loading the truck and were now standing by listening.

"She has your measure, old boy," one of them replied, grinning.

The fox yapped again and then called down below the counter, "Hey, Ali! Come up here a moment and see if you can scare this one."

The upper portion of a huge, tousle-headed, hideous, yet pathetic-looking giant rose slowly from beneath and stared fixedly at Mouche, who stared back. She could not help herself.

Mr. Reynardo performed the introductions: "This is our giant, Alifanfaron—Ali for short. Ali, this is Mouche, and she's crazy about me."

Mouche started to reply indignantly, "I am not," but thought better of it and decided to let it go and see what would happen. The giant seemed to be trying desperately to recall something and finally said in a mild, friendly voice, "Fi-fo-fe . . . No no—fo-fe-fi—— Oh dear. That isn't it either. I never seem to get it straight."

Mouche prompted him, "Fe-fi-fo . . ."

Ali nodded his head. "Of course. And then the last one is fum. But what's the use? I don't really frighten you, do I?"

On an odd impulse Mouche solemnly felt her heart beat for a moment and then replied, "Oh, I'm so sorry. I'm afraid you don't."

The giant said sadly, "Never mind. I'd really rather be

friends. Then I can have my head scratched. Please scratch my head."

Obediently Mouche gently rubbed the wooden head while Ali sighed and pushed slightly against her fingers like a cat. Once more Mouche felt herself strangely moved and even more so when the fox yipped, "Me too, me too," like a child that has been left out of something, and came whipping over and leaned his head against her shoulder.

A battered and paint-shy old Citroën with a luggage rack on the roof and a trunk fastened to the rear drove alongside the booth from out of the darkness, and a fearful and astonishing apparition climbed out.

He was a one-eyed Negro in the tattered remnants of the uniform of a Senegalese line regiment, a wrinkled old man with a large, rubbery face, naked, glistening skull, and a mouthful of gold teeth that testified he might once have known more opulent times.

He wore not a black but a soiled white patch over his blind left eye which gave him a terrifying aspect, though this was belied, however, by an innocent and childlike grin. There were sergeant's stripes on the uniform sleeve and he had an old World War I *képi* on the back of his head. Around his neck was slung a guitar.

He took in the group and shook his head in marvel, chuckling, "Whooeeeee! Who you chasing up this time, Mr. Reynardo? Can't leave you alone two minutes before you go making eyes at something in skirts."

Mr. Reynardo leered at the Senegalese. "You, Golo! Cough up that ten-franc piece I saw you palm when you took up that last collection this evening."

The Senegalese grinned admiringly. "You saw that, Mr. Reynardo? By my life, you don't miss much, do you?" He fished the coin out of his pocket and laid it down on the counter, where the fox immediately pounced on it, saying to Mouche virtuously, "You see? It's good someone is honest around here. Golo, this is a friend of mine by the name of Mouche. We're thinking of getting married. Mouche, meet Golo. He's our orchestra."

Mouche found herself shaking hands solemnly with the Negro, who bowed courteously and carried her hand halfway to his lips as though she were a queen.

Mr. Reynardo rasped, "Break it up. You'll be giving her ideas." Then to Mouche, "By the way, kid, can you sing?"

Mouche replied, "A little. Can you?"

"Oh yes," Mr. Reynardo admitted. "Heroic tenor. And I've got a friend who is a pretty good basso. We could have a trio. Hey, Ali, send the Doc up. Golo, you play something for us."

The giant disappeared to be replaced by a solemn-looking penguin who wore a pince-nez attached to a black ribbon and was introduced by the fox as Dr. Duclos, a member of the academy.

The penguin bowed and murmured, "Charmed, indeed. Forgive the formal clothes. I have just come from the annual dinner of the Anthropofumbling Society."

Golo leaned against the dented wing of the Citroën and fingered the advance ghost of a melody on his guitar, then struck a firm chord and thereafter, without further introduction, Mouche found herself singing the popular Parisian song hit of the moment:

"Va t'en, va t'en, va t'en!
Je ne suis plus ton amant . . ."

She had not much voice, it was true, but there was a softness and an ingenuous earnestness in it, with a slight throaty quality that was young and pleasing and blended astonishingly well with the unctuous but not unmelodious tenor sung by Mr. Reynardo, supported and interlarded by deep basso "poom-pooms" contributed at the proper musical moments by Dr. Duclos.

"Be off, be off, be off!
I am not your lover any more . . .
Another has taken your place . . ."

The music completed the spell under which Mouche found herself and carried her away into this strangest of all strange lands of make-believe into which she had wandered out of the unhappy night.

The song was catching the ears of their neighbors too. The fortuneteller and her husband ceased quarreling and came nearer to listen, their gypsy eyes glistening in the torchlight. The workman and the truck driver were clapping their hands to punctuate the "Va t'en." A passing cabdriver pulled up to the curb and got out. Late home-goers lingered. Other concessionaires came over from nearby pitches which they had been engaged in dismantling. Soon a considerable crowd had formed a semicircle about the dingy little puppet booth.

These were hard, rough people mostly; the night was cold and the hour late, but they too succumbed to the spell of the odd little talking dolls, the music, and the new ingredient that had been added—the waif.

Even this brief space of time had seen a transformation worked in Mouche. The listlessness and despair had been shed. If anything, her gauntness, the hunger-thin frame, and the large, tender, believing eyes shining from the pale countenance added to the attraction as in company with the sly-looking, amorous fox and the pompous, stuffy, overdignified penguin she acted out the verses of the song, playing first to one and then to the other, as though she had really changed lovers.

They ended with a shout and a thump of Golo's guitar, and his hearty chuckle was heard above the applause and bravos of the audience. Mouche did not even notice Golo reach behind the booth for a battered tin poilu's helmet with which he passed swiftly through the crowd, nor the response to his collection in bills and coins, for she was too absorbed with Mr. Reynardo and Dr. Duclos, who were taking elaborate bows.

"You were in excellent voice tonight, my dear Reynardo."

"Permit me to compliment you likewise, friend Duclos."

To Mouche, Reynardo remarked, "You know, I could make something out of you, baby." And Dr. Duclos added importantly, "Your solfège is not at all bad, my child. I say of course that everything is diaphragm control. . . ."

From somewhere in the depths of the booth a bell rang. Mr. Reynardo let out a yelp. "Oops! Supper! Sorry. Nice to have met you, kid. Come on, Doc."

The fox and the penguin disappeared beneath the stage. Golo regarded Mouche for a moment with the sad creamy eyes of an old Negro who had seen much. He said, "Who are you, miss?"

Mouche replied, "Nobody."

"You brought us good luck."

"Did I? I'm glad."

"Where you go now?"

"I don't know."

His question had restored the chill to the night and the feel of the hard-packed earth beneath her feet. The fairy tale was over then. Yet the echoes still lingered and her heart felt strangely light.

Golo nodded. To have no place to go was familiar to him. He said, "You excuse me, miss. I better get things ready to move."

He went to the car and unstrapped the big theatrical trunk from the rear. Someone at Mouche's elbow went "Pssst!" Another half doll occupied the stage, an elderly woman with a pronounced mustache and indignant eyebrows. She was wearing a coverall and mobcap and carried a dustcloth with which she took an occasional wipe at the counter. When Mouche turned to her she first peered furtively to both sides and then addressed her in a hoarse whisper. "Don't trust them." Instantly Mouche was swept back to this other world. "Don't trust whom?" she asked.

"Don't trust anyone. I am a woman, and believe me, I know what I am talking about."

"But they were all so kind . . ." Mouche protested.

"Hah! That's just how they do it. I am Madame Muscat, the concierge, here. I know everything that goes on. You look as though you might be a respectable girl. The things I could tell you . . . They're all a bad lot, and if you take my advice you won't have anything to do with them."

Mouche was not one to listen to gossip, and Madame Muscat was exactly like all the concierges she had ever known.

Nevertheless, she felt a pang at her heart, the kind one ex-periences when ill is spoken of dear friends. She cried, "Oh, surely that can't be so. . . ."

Golo went by carrying the trunk on his shoulders. He paused and said reprovingly: "You oughtn't to say things like that, Madame Muscat. They ain't really so bad. They just young and a little wild." To Mouche he said reassuringly, "Don't you pay her any attention, miss. Wait until I put her in this trunk again. That will keep her quiet."

Madame Muscat gave a little shriek at the threat and ducked quickly beneath the counter as Golo continued on behind the booth.

In her place there appeared then finally one more puppet, an old gentleman who wore square steel-rimmed spectacles, a stocking cap, and leather apron. The expression painted on his face contrived sometimes to be quizzical and friendly; at others, when he moved his head, searching and benign. For a moment he appeared to look right through Mouche. Then in a gentle voice he spoke to her, saying, "Good evening to you. My name is Monsieur Nicholas. I am a maker and mender of toys. My child, I can see you are in trouble. Behind your eyes are many more tears than you have shed."

Mouche's hand flew to her throat because of the ache that had come to lodge there. It had been so long since anyone had called her "child."

Monsieur Nicholas said, "Perhaps you would care to tell me about it."

Golo appeared again. He said, "You tell *him*, miss. He is a good man. Everybody who has troubles tells them to Monsieur Nicholas."

Now the tears came swiftly to Mouche's eyes, and with their flow something loosened inside her so that as she stood there in the garish light before the shabby puppet booth and the single animated wooden doll listening so attentively to her the story of her trials and failures poured from her in moving innocence, for she could not have confessed it thus to any human.

When she had reached the end of her unhappy tale, Monsieur Nicholas concluded for her, ". . . And so you were going to throw yourself into the Seine tonight."

Mouche stared, marveling. "How did you know?"

"It was not hard to tell. There is nothing to seek for one as young as you at the bottom of the river."

"But, Monsieur Nicholas—what shall I do? Where shall I go?"

The puppet bowed his head as he reflected gravely for a moment, a tiny hand held to his brow. Then he tilted his head to one side and asked, "Would you care to come with us?"

"Come with you? Oh, could I? Do you suppose I could?" It was as though suddenly a vista of heaven had opened for

Mouche. For she loved them already, all of these queer, compelling little individuals who each, in a few brief moments, had captured her imagination or tugged at her heartstrings. To make believe forever—or as the day was long—to escape from reality into this unique world of fantasy . . . She held out her arms in supplication and cried, "Oh, Monsieur Nicholas! Would you really take me with you?"

The puppet contemplated silently for a moment and then said, "You must ask Poil de Carotte. Officially, he manages the show. Good-by."

The stage remained empty for an appreciable time. Then an insouciant whistling was heard and Poil de Carotte appeared bouncing jauntily along the counter, looking nowhere in particular. As though surprised, he said, "Oh, hello, Mouche, you still here?"

The girl was uncertain how to approach him. He was mercurial. His mood now seemed to be quite different. She ventured: "Monsieur Nicholas said . . ."

Carrot Top nodded. "Oh yes. I heard about it."

"May I come, please, dear Carrot Top?"

The doll with the worried expression looked her over. "When you ask so prettily it is hard to refuse. . . . After all, it was I who discovered you, wasn't it? However, if you come with us you wouldn't always be telling me what to do, would you? You know, I have a lot of responsibility with this show."

"Oh no . . ."

"But you'd look after us, wouldn't you?"

"If you'd let me . . ."

"Sew on buttons and things?"

"Darn socks . . ."

"We have no feet," Carrot Top said severely. "That's the first thing you'll have to learn."

"Then I'd knit you mittens."

Carrot Top nodded. "That would be nice. We've never had mittens. There'd be no money, you know."

"I wouldn't care . . ."

"Very well then . . . In that case you can come."

"Oh, Carrot Top!"

"Mouche!"

Mouche never knew exactly how it happened, but suddenly she was close to the booth, weeping with joy, and Carrot Top had both his arms around her neck and was patting her cheek with one of his little wooden hands. He wailed, "Mouche, don't cry. I always meant you to come. I only had to pretend because I'm the manager. . . . Welcome to Poil de Carrotte and the family of Capitaine Coq."

From below there sounded the sardonic yapping of the fox and the shrill voice of Gigi: "Why does she have to come with us? There isn't enough for everybody now." Madame Muscat whisked across the stage once, croaking, "Remember, I warned

34

you." Ali arose and rumbled, "Gee, I'm glad. I need looking after because I'm so stupid. Scratch my head."

Carrot Top suddenly became efficient. "Not now, Ali. We've got to get cracking. Golo . . . Golo, where are you?"

"Right here, little boss." The Senegalese appeared from behind the booth.

"Mouche is coming with us. Find her a place in the car."

The Negro shouted, "Bravo! That's mighty good luck for us. I find her a place in the car."

"Then come back and strike the set, Golo."

"Yes, sir, little boss. Strike the set. I'll do that. You come along with me, miss, and I fix you right up." He picked up Mouche's valise and went with her to the Citroën, where he stowed it in the luggage boot in the rear. Then he looked into the back seat of the car, which was buried beneath pieces of old clothing, newspapers, maps, bits of costumes for the puppets, and props, packages, a bottle of beer, a half-eaten loaf of bread, tools, and a spare tin of petrol along with other masculine litter.

Golo began a futile rummaging. "Don't look like they's much room, but . . ."

Mouche took over. "Never mind, Golo. I promised Carrot Top I'd look after things. I'll have it tidied up in no time."

As she worked, Mouche sang, "Va t'en, va t'en, va t'en . . ." humming the melody happily to herself. But through her head were running new words to the old song: "Go away, Death!

You are not my lover any longer. I have found a new one called Life. It is to him I shall always be faithful . . ."

She cleared a small space for herself on the seat, folded the clothing and the maps, wrapped the bread and a piece of sausage she found, stowed the costumes carefully where they would not get dirty, and while she was at it gave a good brushing and cleaning to the old car, which in a sense was to be her future home, one that she would share with Carrot Top, Reynardo, Ali, Madame Muscat and Gigi, Golo and all the rest.

So bemused and enchanted was she that not once did she give a thought to that other who would also be there, the unseen puppeteer who animated the seven dolls.

When she had finished it was only the spare tin of petrol that had defeated her, and she emerged from the car searching for Golo to ask his advice.

Yet when Mouche discovered him nearby she found herself unable to call or even speak, so strange and ominous was the sight that met her eyes.

For the booth with all its endearing occupants had vanished from the spot it had occupied and now lay flat, a compact pile of board, canvas, oilcloth, and painted papier-mâché, tarpaulined and roped by Golo, who was finishing the job with the sure movements of long practice. None of the puppets was in sight and reposed presumably in the trunk that stood nearby.

But the pole with the flaming gasoline torch was still there and against it leaned a man Mouche had not seen before. He was clad in corduroy trousers, rough shoes, and was wearing a roll-neck sweater under some kind of old army fatigue jacket. A stocking cap was pulled down on one side of his head and a cigarette hung from his lips.

In the wavering light it was not possible to judge his age, but his attitude and the expression on his face and mouth were cold, cynical, and mocking. His eyes were fixed on Mouche and she could see their glitter reflecting the torchlight.

It was like a chill hand laid upon her heart, for there was no warmth or kindliness in the figure lounging against the pole, his fists pressed deeply into the pockets of his jacket. The shine of his eyes was hostile and the droop of the cigarette from his lips contemptuous.

Mouche, in her marrow, knew that this was the puppet master, the man who had animated the little creatures that had laid such an enchantment upon her, yet she was filled with dread. For a moment even she hoped that somehow this was not he, the master of the dolls, but some other, a pitchman, a laborer, or lounger from a neighboring concession.

Golo, straightening up from his task, looked from one to the other, the silent man, the frightened girl, and presented them to one another elaborately, as though they had never met before, as though the man had not been able to look through his one-way curtain behind which he sat as he gave life and voice to his puppets, and study each curve and hollow of the girl's face and every line of her thin body.

"Miss Mouche, this is Capitaine Coq," Golo explained, and then turned to the man, who had not stirred. "Capitaine, this here is Miss Mouche. Carrot Top, he find her walking along in the dark by herself, crying, and he stop her and have a talk with her. Then Mr. Reynardo, he find out she a pretty damn good singer, and Monsieur Nicholas, he come up and ask maybe she like to come along with us, after that old gossip Madame Muscat, she try to make trouble. Then Carrot Top, he say okay she can come along with the show. I think that very good luck for everybody." He paused, satisfied. Golo was convinced that the little creatures thought and acted as individuals and that the puppeteer was not privy to what they said and did or what transpired among them.

Mouche, too, had been under the same spell, and the presence of the man confused and alarmed her and increased the turmoil of her emotions.

The man introduced as Capitaine Coq moved his eyes slightly so as to take in Golo and rasped, "Well, what do you expect me to do about it? What did Carrot Top tell you to do?"

"To get the gear on the car, Monsieur le Capitaine."

"Well, then, get on with it. And you drive. I want to get some sleep."

"Get the gear onto the car. Okay, sir." Golo picked up the heavy bundle but was slow in moving. The Captain barked "*Allez!*" at him and helped him with a kick.

Golo did not exclaim or protest. Mouche thought she would die of shame and sadness because of the manner in which the Negro scuttled under the impetus of the blow, like an animal —or a human who has well learned the futility of protest against cruelty.

Reality as cold as the night engulfed Mouche. The man's personality and harshness were as acrid as the stench from the smoking flare above his head. Now he turned his calculating stare upon Mouche and for the first time spoke directly to her. He did not remove the cigarette from his lips, and it hung there, remaining horrifyingly motionless when he talked, for he had the professional ventriloquist's trick of speaking without moving his lips when he wished.

"You, Mouche! Come here."

She felt herself hypnotized. She was unable to resist moving slowly toward him. When she stood in front of him he looked her up and down.

"You needn't waste any sympathy on Golo," he said, again having read her. "He has a better life than he would have elsewhere. Now you listen to me. . . ." He paused, and the cigarette end glowed momentarily. Mouche felt herself trembling. "You can stay with us as long as you behave yourself and help with the act. If you don't, I'll kick you out, no matter what Carrot Top says. Carrot Top likes you. Rey and Dr. Duclos seem to think you can sing. That baby bleat of yours makes me sick, but it pulled in the francs from that crowd tonight, and that's all I care. Now get into the back of that car. You may have some bread and sausage if you're hungry. But not a sound out of you. March!"

Had she had her suitcase in her possession, Mouche would have turned and fled. But it was locked now in the luggage boot and she had a woman's inability to part with her possessions no matter how wretched they might be. And besides, where was she to go? Not the river any more, at the bottom of which writhed eels and crayfish, as Carrot Top had warned her.

Half blinded with tears, Mouche turned away and obeyed him.

She heard the scraping and thudding on the roof as Golo fastened the dismantled puppet booth to the rack and then tied the trunk on behind.

Capitaine Coq got into the front seat, pulled his stocking cap over his eyes, and went to sleep. The car, guided by Golo, moved off, crossing the bridge and turning north at the Porte de Neuilly, sought the highroad to Rheims.

Huddled in the back seat, Mouche dried her tears and nibbled on the bread and sausage. She managed to derive comfort from the fact that safe in the trunk behind her, tarpaulined against inclement weather, were all the little creatures who had seemed to like her. And she remembered that even Capitaine Coq had spoken of them in the third person, as though their lives were their own.

Just before she fell asleep she felt the trunk scrape against the rear of the car and she smiled, thinking of Poil de Carotte bowed beneath his managerial worries, the hypocritical but lovable fox, the unhappy giant, the sulky golden-haired girl, the pompous but friendly penguin, the gossipy concierge who at bottom was a woman who could be trusted, and the kind and touching mender of broken toys. Surely she would be meeting them all again. . . .

Part Two

The real name of the man who billed himself as Capitaine Coq was Michel Peyrot, and he was bred out of the gutters of Paris, the same which in an earlier age had spawned Villon.

His had been a life without softness or pity. He had never known his father. When he was six his mother, who earned her living on the street, was murdered. Michel was taken by a carnival family. His foster mother, a worn-out soubrette, augmented her income by obliging clients behind the tent after the performance; his foster father was a fire eater in the freak show and was rarely sober.

When Michel was twelve, the fire eater engaged in a duel with a rival from another fair but, being drunk, miscalculated the amount of petrol he could store in his cheeks to blow out from his mouth in flames. Swallowing some which became ignited simultaneously, he died horribly of internal combustion. His wife, already undermined with disease, did not survive him long, and at thirteen Michel was again alone in the world.

By the time he was fifteen he was a little savage practiced in all of the cruel arts and swindles of the street fairs and cheap carnivals. Now at thirty-five he was handsome in a rakish way, with wiry, reddish hair, wide-spaced gray eyes in a pale face, and a virile crooked nose wrinkled still further by a blow that had flattened it during a brief experiment with pugilism and which, with a sensuous mouth, gave him something of the look of a satyr.

Throughout his life no one had ever been kind to him, or gentle, and he paid back the world in like. Wholly cynical, he had no regard or respect for man, woman, child, or God. Not at any time he could remember in his thirty-five years of existence had he ever loved anything or anyone. He looked upon women as conveniences that his appetite demanded and, after he had used them, abandoned them or treated them badly. Why he had picked up the thin, wretched bit of flotsam known as Mouche he could not have told. Indeed, he would have insisted that it was not he at all who had added her to his queer family, but the members of that group themselves, Carrot Top, Mr. Reynardo, Madame Muscat, and Monsieur Nicholas, who had made the decision.

For in spite of the fact that it was he who sat behind the one-way curtain in the booth, animated them and supplied their seven voices, the puppets frequently acted strangely and determinedly as individuals over whom he had no control. Michel never had bothered to reflect greatly over this phenomenon but had simply accepted it as something that was so and which, far from interfering with the kind of life he was accustomed to living, brought him a curious kind of satisfaction.

Growing up with the people of the carnival acts, Michel had learned juggling, sword-swallowing, and leaping on the trampolin, but it was in ventriloquism that he became the most proficient.

The lives of the puppets had begun when Michel Peyrot was a prisoner of the Germans during the war and in their camps had a kind of postgraduate course in all that was base in human nature.

In this evil period of an evil life he first carved and clad the seven puppets, brought them to life for the entertainment of his fellow prisoners, and made the discovery that more and more they refused to speak the obscenities and vulgarities that make soldiers laugh, but instead were becoming individuals with lives of their own.

During those times that he sat hidden in the puppet booth, Michel Peyrot was not, but the seven were. Golo, the derelict Senegalese, understood this paradox perfectly. To him it was simply the primitive jungle magic by which his spirit was enabled to leave the body and enter into other objects which then became imbued with his life. But there was yet another manifestation of which Michel Peyrot was unaware, and that was that under the scheme of creation it was not possible for a man to be wholly wicked and live a life entirely devoted to evil.

If Carrot Top, Gigi, and Ali the giant were restoring to him the childhood of which he had been robbed, or Reynardo, Dr. Duclos, Madame Muscat, and Monsieur Nicholas the means by which he could escape from himself, Michel was not consciously aware of it. Often he was cynically amused at the things done and the sentiments expressed by his creations, for they were completely foreign to him.

Yet the habit of the puppet booth grew, and when the war

ended and he returned to France, Michel Peyrot became Capitaine Coq, and with Golo, whom he had found starving in the prison camp, as slave, orchestra, and factotum took to the road.

The last night of the fair outside the Porte de Neuilly in Paris it had been the experienced and cynical eye of Capitaine Coq that had instantly detected the despairing shoulder slope and the blind, suicide walk of the unhappy girl with the straw valise, but it had been Poil de Carotte, the puppet with the red hair and pointed ears, who had saved her, for Coq would not have given a fig for a whole troupe of despairing girls marching single file into the Seine. He had looked upon women and death and dead women unmoved. But it amused him to let Carrot Top and the others deal with the girl as they wished.

Nevertheless, once the strange little play had begun and the seven had proceeded independently with their work of capturing her, Coq's sharp showman's instincts had been quick to recognize the value of this trusting child speaking seriously and with complete belief across the booth to the inhabitants thereof. Whoever or whatever she was, she was possessed of that indefinable something that bridges the gap separating audience and performer and touches the heart of the beholder. He had noted her effect upon the hardened crowd of pitchmen, laborers, and fellow rascals who had gathered about his booth. If the girl could be taught to work thus spontaneously with his family, standing out in front of the counter, she might become a definite business asset. If not, he could always kick her out or abandon her.

But there was one more quality that had attracted him in her, as he had peered through the scrim of the blind curtain and seen her pinched shoulders, hollow cheeks, dark unhappy eyes, and snow-white, blue-veined temples beneath the short-cut black hair, or rather which had exasperated him and roused all of the bitterness and hatred of which he had so great a supply. This was her innocence and essential purity. Capitaine Coq was the mortal enemy of innocence. It was the one trait in human beings, man or woman, boy or girl, that he could not bear. He would, if he could, have corrupted the whole world.

In the back of the car Mouche had slept the sleep of mental and physical exhaustion. When she awoke it was morning, and she was alone. All of the panic of the night before returned overwhelmingly and she sprang from the machine, looking about her fearfully. But the bright sunlight and the surroundings helped to dissipate some of her fears. The dilapidated vehicle was parked in a tangled area behind booths and concessions of yet another fair. In the background she saw the twin towers of the damaged cathedral of Rheims.

There was a water pump nearby and she went to it and washed her face, the cold water helping to clear her head.

When she ventured through the tangle of guy wires and stays supporting a nearby tent, she heard suddenly a voice with a familiar rasp: "Hola, Mouche!"

She edged through to the street on which the fair fronted. It was Mr. Reynardo. The booth that she had seen only by torch flare the night before was standing once more. It looked shabby in the morning light. But there was no disputing that Mr. Reynardo was a fine figure of an impudent red fox.

He whistled at her, opened his jaws, and asked, "Wash your face, baby?"

"Of course," Mouche replied, and then asked pointedly, "Did you?"

"No, but don't tell anyone. I think I got away with it." He whipped below and was replaced by Carrot Top, who held a hundred-franc note in his two hands. He said:

"Oh, hello, Mouche. Sleep all right?"

"Oh yes, thank you. I think so." The most delicious relief pervaded her. Here they were again, her little friends of the night before. How natural it seemed to be standing there talking to them.

Carrot Top piped, "Go get yourself some bread and cheese for your breakfast," and handed her the note. "There's an épicerie just down the street. I've still got a lot to do to get the show ready. And bring back the change."

As she turned to go, somebody behind her went "Psssssst!"

She looked around and saw Mr. Reynardo in a corner of the booth, motioning to her with his head. She went to him and he stretched his snout up to her ear and whispered hoarsely, "There needn't be any change."

Mouche asked, "What do you mean, Mr. Reynardo?"

The fox contrived a wicked leer. "Call me Rey. Shhhh . . . Everybody knows prices are up. Say breakfast cost more and keep the difference. But remember, it was my idea. Fifty-fifty, kid . . ."

Mouche shook her head as earnestly as though she were reproving a child. "But, Rey . . . Really! That isn't honest."

"Ha, ha!" yipped the fox. "Maybe not, but it's the only way you'll get any money out of this outfit. Don't say I didn't tip you."

When Mouche returned from her breakfast and with thirty francs left over, Carrot Top and Gigi, the ingenue, were holding the stage. The leprechaun was trying to comb her hair, the angle of his head giving a worried and concentrated expression to his face. A half dozen people were standing about, watching.

Carrot Top looked up. "Oh, back again, Mouche? Had your breakfast?"

Mouche replied politely, "Yes, thank you. And here's your change."

Carrot Top nodded absently, took the money, disappeared beneath the counter with it, and reappeared almost immediately, saying, "I'm trying to do Gigi's hair. It's full of mare's-nests."

Gigi whined sulkily, "It is not. He's hurting me."

"Bird's nests, you mean," Mouche corrected. "Here, let me help. Girls know how to do that ever so much better."

Carrot Top looked severe. "Men make the best hairdressers ——" he announced, but surrendered the comb to Mouche, who applied herself gently to reducing the snarls in Gigi's golden wig.

Gigi commanded, "I want braids. I'm tired of all that hair in my eyes. Braid my hair, Mouche."

"Certainly, Gigi," Mouche acquiesced. "And then we'll wind it about your ears in two buns, Bretonne fashion."

Unself-consciously, as though there were no one else watching, she set about combing and separating the hair into strands and then began to weave the braids, singing as she did so an ancient Breton hair-braiding song that for centuries mothers had sung to their little daughters to keep them quiet during the ceremony. It went:

"First,
    One and three
        then
    Three and two
        then
    Two and one,

NOW—

    One and two
        and
    Three and one
        and
    Two and one . . ."

It had a simple, repetitive, hypnotic melody and Golo, appearing from behind the booth with his guitar, fingered the strings softly for a moment and picked it up. Dr. Duclos appeared with some sheet music which he read earnestly through the pince-nez affixed to his beak and contributed basso "poom-pooms." Gigi beat time with her hands. In no time there was a fascinated and enchanted crowd, ten-deep, gathered about the booth.

When the hair was braided and bunned, Gigi and Dr. Duclos went away and Carrot Top, taking the empty stage, explained the plot of their play. He is in love with Gigi, but the girl is being compelled by her greedy mother, Madame Muscat, to marry wealthy, windy old Dr. Duclos. Carrot Top's friend Reynardo sends the giant Alifanfaron to abduct Gigi, but being likewise in the employ of Dr. Duclos, the double-crossing fox arranges for the giant to steal Madame Muscat while he makes love to Gigi instead.

Into this plot, without further preparation, Mouche was

drawn by the puppets to explain, guide, mother, scold, keeping their secrets, sharing others with the audience, while playing a variety of roles, a maid, Mr. Reynardo's secretary, Dr. Duclos's sister, a friend of Madame Muscat . . .

She had a quick wit for situations, but above all she had the ability to forget herself and become wholly immersed in the goings on. Because she believed so completely in the little creatures, she had the unique power of transferring this belief to the audience and, with a look, a laugh, or a single tender passage between herself and one of the puppets, transport the watchers away from the hard-packed earth on which they stood and into the world of make-believe, where the ordinary rules of life and living did not obtain.

Before the little play was over, all concerned had changed sides so often that Monsieur Nicholas had to appear to untangle them and at the finish, to great applause, Carrot Top and Gigi, Dr. Duclos and Madame Muscat and Ali and Mouche were paired off, for the poor giant made such a muddle of things that Mouche had to take him under her wing and he proceeded to fall desperately and moon-calf in love with her.

That day the collection made by Golo far surpassed anything Coq and his family had earned heretofore, and the puppeteer took a room in a cheap hotel for himself and a servant's room upstairs for Mouche. Golo was still relegated to sleep in the car and watch over the puppets. He did not mind this, for he preferred to be with them.

And that night all three ate a good supper at the inn with red wine, of which Coq drank heavily. The drink did not make him mellower, but on the contrary still more scornful and contemptuous of Mouche.

He ate grossly, ignoring her presence, but once when he felt her large eyes upon him in the uneasy silence that lay over their table like an oasis in the center of the noisy, smoky bistro, he looked up from his eating and snarled at her, "What the devil got into you this afternoon when Carrot Top asked you what to do to win Gigi and fly away with him in his helicopter? You stood there frozen and staring like an animal. Why didn't you tell him?"

It was not the reproof but the sudden shifting of the base of this new and marvelous world into which she had been ushered that disturbed Mouche. It was as though there had been an unwarranted intrusion by an outsider.

"Why," she explained carefully, "Carrot Top doesn't want to be told what to do. He made me promise before he let me come along that I was never to interfere with him. And besides," she concluded after a moment of reflection, "he doesn't really love Gigi at all, because——"

She broke off in alarm, for Capitaine Coq was staring at her, his face now flushed dark with rage.

54

"What makes you think you know who Carrot Top loves or doesn't love, you milk-faced little fool?"

For a moment Mouche thought the redheaded man was about to hurl his plate of food in her face.

She said, "I . . . I'm sorry. I really don't know . . . I suppose I just guessed. I won't do it again."

The fury did not abate from the countenance of Coq, but he did not speak to her again and instead took it out on Golo, shouting at him, "What are you lingering for, you black monkey? Haven't you stuffed yourself enough? Get away back to the car before everything is pilfered. . . ."

They continued to eat and drink in heavy silence until Mouche gathered the courage to speak to him again. In her simple, gentle way she asked, "Monsieur le Capitaine, why are you always so angry?"

He laid down his knife and fork and stared long at her out of his cold hard eyes. "Because you are a fool," he replied finally, "and I have no time for fools, particularly women."

Mouche was not hurt, for she was used to living where men were outspoken. And besides, she did not think she was clever or, since the disasters that had happened to her, even talented any longer. Impulsively she reached over and placed her hand upon his in a sweet conciliatory gesture, saying, "Dear Capitaine Coq—why cannot you be as kind and patient with me as Carrot Top, Dr. Duclos, and Mr. Reynardo? I am sure they thought I was very stupid at times today, but they never showed it."

The touch of her gentle fingers seemed to sting Capitaine Coq, and he snatched his hand away. "Because your staring eyes and whining innocence make me sick."

The attack was so savage that the tears came to Mouche's eyes and she nodded silently.

"As for them," Capitaine Coq continued, draining his glass, "it is no concern of mine what they do. Get along with them, if you know what is good for you, during working hours. And keep out of my way at other times. Understood?"

Mouche nodded again. "I'll try."

Yet in spite of the harshness of Capitaine Coq, which had the effect only of moving her to a kind of pity for him, for he seemed to be so wretched in his furies, the week of the street fair in Rheims was one of the happiest times Mouche had ever known.

The warmth of her relationship with the seven puppets seemed to grow by leaps and bounds, and soon she was familiar with their characteristics, their strengths and weaknesses: the striving and ambitious little Carrot Top with the soaring imagination which always wished to brush aside earth-bound obstacles and yet was tied down by the responsibility for all the others and the running of the show; the pompous, long-winded, fatuous Dr. Duclos, the prototype of every self-satisfied stuffed shirt, who still in his bumbling way was kind; and the vain, foolish, self-centered ingenue Gigi, who, of all the little dolls, was not.

Most dependent upon her was Alifanfaron, the giant, who frightened no one and was so kindhearted and slow-witted that everyone took advantage of him. He looked pathetically to Mouche for help and protection, and some of the most charming passages took place between the ugly, fearful-looking monster and the young girl who mothered him.

She got on best with Madame Muscat, for the madame was a woman who had seen life and buried husbands, understood men and felt that women should stick together for mutual protection. She was always Mouche's ally with advice or an aphorism, or a bit of useful gossip as to what was going on backstage or below the counter, that mysterious domain where the puppets dwelt.

But if Mouche had had to select a favorite of them all, it would have been Mr. Reynardo. He touched her most deeply because he was sly, wicked, not quite honest, knew it, and wished and tried, but not too fervently, to be better.

He amused her too. He baited and teased her and sometimes worked up little intrigues against her with the others, but when it came right down to it he also seemed to love her the most and feel the deepest need for her affection. Much of his yapping was bravado, and the moments when Mouche felt almost unbearably touched and happy were when from time to time cracks appeared in his armor of cynicism and through them she caught glimpses of the small child within wanting to be forgiven and loved.

Though he was her friend and counselor, Mouche remained a little in awe of Monsieur Nicholas, the mender of toys, for he was a dispenser of impartial justice as well as kindness. His glance through his square spectacles always seemed to penetrate her and reach to her innermost secret thoughts.

Childlike, too, but in the primitive fashion backed by the dark lore of his race, was Golo. He was indeed the slave who served the puppets and, now that Mouche had become as one of them, hers too. He was versed in the mechanics of the show, yet they meant nothing to him. One moment he could be behind the booth assisting Capitaine Coq in a costume change for one of the puppets, handing him props or hanging the dolls in proper order, head down so that Coq could thrust his hands into them quickly for those lightning appearances and disappearances of the characters, and the next, out front with Mouche, he looked upon them as living, breathing creatures.

The belief in the separate existence of these little people was even more basic with Mouche, for it was a necessity to her and a refuge from the storms of life with which she had been unable to cope.

If fundamentally she must have been aware that it was Coq who animated them, she managed to obliterate the thought. For how could one reconcile the man and his creations? And further, she rarely saw Capitaine Coq enter or leave the booth, for he was moody and mysterious in his comings and goings. Sometimes he would sit inside for as long as an hour in the early morning or even late at night, without giving a sign of his presence there until suddenly one or more of his puppets would appear on-stage.

All orders were given, all business directed through Carrot Top, all rehearsals conducted, new songs learned, plots and bits of business discussed with the puppets, until conversing with them became second nature to Mouche and it became almost impossible for her to associate this odd family of such diverse characters with the pale, bitter man who was their creator.

When the week of the fair was at an end in Rheims, they moved on to Sedan for three days and thence to Montmédy and Metz, for that year it was Capitaine Coq's intention to tour northeastern France and Alsace until the cold weather drove them south.

One night, without warning, Capitaine Coq emerged, half drunk and amorous, from the taproom of the sordid little inn on the outskirts of the city where they were quartered.

It was late. There were no women about, the regulars having long since paired off or disappeared. He bethought himself then of a piece of property he considered belonged to him, the thin girl asleep upstairs in the narrow bedroom under the eaves.

It was time, he thought as well, that the little ninny learned something and became a woman. And besides, since they were traveling together, it would be cheaper if henceforth they occupied one room—and perhaps, if she was not a stick, convenient too.

But there was yet another darker purpose that sent him prowling up the stairs that led to the attic chamber. It was the fact that her gentleness, innocence, and purity of heart were a perpetual affront to him, the kind of man he was and the life that he led. It had been worming him ever since he had first laid eyes on her. Now he could no longer bear it unless he pulled her down to his level and made her as he was.

He tiptoed to her door, bent and listened for a moment, then, turning the handle swiftly, he whipped inside with the furtive speed of one of his own puppets and closed the door behind him.

When Mouche awoke the next morning, the sunshine was pouring in through the dormer window as if to deny the nightmare that had happened to her. She had thought she would not sleep that night, or ever sleep again. Yet, somehow, oblivion had come, and now the day.

She got out of bed and went to the window which looked on to the rear courtyard of the inn, where a dog lolloped, a pig lay in the mud, chickens picked at the ground, and ducks and a goose waddled through puddles of dirty water.

They reminded her of her childhood and the farmyards of her village in Brittany, and she wondered how she could stand there so calmly contemplating them and the memories they aroused, she who would never be as a child again.

Mouche had neither protested nor resisted Capitaine Coq's act of darkness. Out of the darkness he had come, in darkness taken her, and to darkness returned, leaving her bruised, defiled, and ashamed.

Startled out of her sleep by his presence, she had recognized him when a shaft of moonlight had fallen across his pale face with the crinkled nose, draining the red from his hair, turning it to purple.

For an instant her heart had leaped, for she thought that perhaps he loved her, and she would not have denied him.

But there was no love in his eyes or in his heart; no whisper came from his lips, and too late she knew what was afoot. It would have been of no use to cry out. Besides, where could she have escaped to, naked, alone, friendless and penniless in a strange inn? He was there before she could make a move, intruding himself into her room, her consciousness, her bed, and then her person.

The brutality of his passion brought her close to a climax of her own, one of seemingly unbearable grief, anguish, and pain, and once she had murmured his name, "Michel," piteously. She thought that surely she would die.

Then he was gone at last, leaving her shamed to death because he had abused her so callously without loving her, weeping miserably with humiliation and hurt because of his cynical contempt for her, the disgusting arrogance and carelessness of his possession of her person. He had not given her a single kindly glance, or caress, or kiss; no word, no gentleness. He had left not a solitary ray of hope to illuminate the despair that engulfed her, that within his strong, imprisoning, goatish body there beat a human heart.

And she was the more shamed because of the instinct that told her that, despite the horror and brutality, she had yielded and the act and the moment might make her forever his.

These were the black memories, her thoughts and fears that morning as she washed and clad the body that was no longer a citadel, and prepared to face what the day would bring.

And yet the miracle occurred again, for that day was yet like any other, except, if anything, the troupe was still kinder and friendlier to her.

Carrot Top greeted her with a shrill cry of delight when she arrived at the booth. "Hey, Mouche! Where you been? Do you know what? There's sausage for breakfast. Golo! Give Mouche her sausage."

As the Senegalese appeared from behind the booth with

garlic country sausage and fresh bread on a paper plate, Mr. Reynardo popped up from below with a large piece in his jaws and thrust it at her, saying, "Here. I saved a piece of mine for you. And you *know* how I love sausage. . . ."

Mouche said, "Oh, Rey. Did you really? That was sweet of you. . . ."

From below a protesting rumble was heard, and as Carrot Top vanished Alifanfaron appeared. "Say, who stole that piece of sausage I was saving for Mouche?"

Shocked at such effrontery, Mouche cried, "Rey, you *didn't* . . ." But the attitude of guilt of the fox condemned him. She said severely, memory of all her own troubles fading, "Rey, give it back to Ali at once. There. Now, Ali, you may give it to me."

The giant presented it. "It's only because I'm so stupid. Rey said he just wanted to borrow it to see if it was as big as his."

Mouche took it from him, leaned over, and kissed the side of his cheek. "Poor, dear Ali," she said. "Never you mind. It's better to be trusting than to have no principles at all like some people around here. . . ."

Reynardo had the grace to look abashed and flattened himself like a dog at the end of the counter. He said, "I tried to save you a piece of mine, honestly I did, Mouche, but it got eaten."

The girl regarded him ruefully. "Oh, Rey . . ." she cried, but there was tenderness in her voice as well as reproof. How had it happened so quickly that the iron bands that had clamped about her heart were easing, the sadness that had weighed her down was lifting? The play was on again.

Like a flash, at the first indication that she might be relenting, Reynardo whipped across the stage and with a hangdog look snuggled his head against her neck and shoulder. Madame Muscat made a brief appearance at the far side of the booth with a small feather duster and dusted the proscenium arch vigorously.

"I warned you, didn't I? You can't trust him for a minute." But she did not say who was not to be trusted. "When you've buried as many husbands as I have . . ." she began, and then vanished without concluding. Carrot Top reappeared, clutching a pale blue thousand-franc note.

"For you, Mouche," he said. "Salary for last week."

Mouche said, "Oh, Carrot Top, really? But ought you? I mean I never . . ."

"It's all right," the leprechaun replied. "We held a meeting this morning and voted you a share. Dr. Duclos presided. His speech from the chair lasted forty-seven minutes. . . ."

A crowd began to collect at the sight of a young girl in earnest conversation with a doll—the day's work began. . . .

All that summer and into the fall they trouped through

eastern France and Alsace, slowly working southward, moving from town to town, sometimes part of a street fair, carnival, or kermess, at others setting up the booth in the market place or square of small villages en route in the country without so much as a by-your-leave from the police or local authorities.

When these officials came demanding permits they found themselves disconcertingly having to deal with Carrot Top, Mr. Reynardo, Madame Muscat, or Dr. Duclos, with Mouche endeavoring to help with the explanations, and usually their charm won the day and they were allowed to remain.

Since by virtue of Mouche's advent the lean days were over, there was always a bed in an inn, cheap hotel, or farmhouse with a room to spare and sometimes the luxury even of a bath at night after a day spent in the hot sun. Only now Capitaine Coq no longer bothered to engage two rooms but simply shared one and the bed in it with Mouche.

Thus Mouche, without realizing it, was possessed by him both by day and by night.

The days continued to be an enduring enchantment, the nights an everlasting torment, whether he used her for his pleasure or turned his back upon her without a word and fell into heavy sleep, leaving her lying there trembling. Sometimes he came to the room in a stupor, barely able to stand after hours of drinking in the taproom. When this happened, Mouche looked after him, undressed him, got him into bed, and when he cursed or moaned and tossed during the night she got up to give him water to drink or place a wet cloth upon his head.

Capitaine Coq was drinking to excess because he had impaled himself upon the horns of a strange and insoluble dilemma and he did not know what to do, except consume wine until all sensation and memory were gone.

On the one hand he was taking all that he wanted or needed from Mouche. She was a growing asset to the show and he was beginning to make money. Further, she was a captive bedmate for whom he need feel no responsibility. But on the other he had made the discovery that while he had indeed been able to ravage her physically, he had never succeeded in destroying her innocence.

He hungered to annihilate it even though at the same time he knew that this was the very quality that drew the audiences and communicated itself to them. Wishing her as soiled and hardened as he was, he debauched her at night and then willy-nilly restored her in the daytime through the medium of the love of the seven dolls, so that phoenix-like she arose each day from the ashes of abuse of the night before, whether it was a tongue-lashing, or a beating, or to be used like a woman of the streets. She was rendered each time as soft and dewy-eyed, as innocent and trusting as she had been the night he had first encountered her on the outskirts of Paris.

The more cruelly he treated her, the kindlier and more friendly to her were the puppets the next morning. He seemed to have lost all control over them.

As for Mouche, she lived in a turmoil of alternating despair and entrancing joy.

One night in Besançon, in a horrible, culminating attempt to break her, Coq appeared in their room with a slut he had picked up in the tavern. They were both drunk.

He switched on the light and stood there looking down at her while she roused herself and sat up. "Get up and get out," he commanded.

She did not understand and sat there staring.

"Get out. I'm sick of you."

She still could not understand what he meant. "But, Michel . . . Where am I to go?"

"To the devil, for all I care. Hurry up and get out. We want that bed. . . ."

That night Mouche reached a new depth of shame and humiliation as she dressed beneath the mocking eyes of the drab and went out of the room, leaving them there. She thought again of dying but was so confused she no longer knew how to die. For a time she wandered about in a daze through the streets, not knowing where she was going.

Then she came upon the Citroën. Golo was sitting at the wheel, smoking a cigarette, his white patch standing out in the light of the street lamp. He appeared to be waiting for her. He got out and took her by the arm.

"You come here and rest, Miss Mouche," he said. He had seen Capitaine Coq go in with the woman and Mouche emerge from the inn and had followed her. He opened the rear door and she climbed in, unseeing, and slumped onto the seat. Golo drove to the nearby fairgrounds and parked. The chimes of the musical clock of Besançon announced the hour of three. Mouche began to weep.

Golo reached back and took her small thin hand in his callused mahogany paw with the fingers hard and scaly from the steel strings of the guitar. But his grip was infinitely tender and his voice even more so as he said, "Do not cry, my little one. . . ." Only it sounded even more beautiful and touching in the soft Senegal French, "Ne pleurez pas, ma petite. Ca fait vous mal aux jolies yeux."

Mouche continued to weep as though she would never be able to cease.

Golo got out of the car, was absent for a moment, and then returned. "Mouche," he called gently. "Miss Mouche. You look here. Please, Miss Mouche, you look. . . ."

The insistence of the soft pleading reached through to Mouche. She took her hands from her face and did as she was bidden. She stared, unbelieving, for a moment. Carrot Top and Mr. Reynardo were looking at her over the top of the front seat.

"Carrot Top! Rey! Oh, my darlings . . ." Mouche cried, her heart near to bursting.

The two stared at her woodenly. Between them shone the face of Golo like the mask of an ancient African god carved out of ebony, but an oddly compassionate god. He said sadly, "They not talk for me, Miss Mouche. But they love you. That's why I brought them here, so you remember that. They always love you."

Mouche reached over and took the two puppets from his hands and cradled the empty husks in her arms, and they brought her comfort until her sorely tried spirit rebelled in an outcry that came from her depths, "But why does he hate me so, Golo? Golo, why is he so cruel, why is he so evil?"

The Senegalese reflected before he replied, "He bewitched. His spirit go out from him. Another come in. Golo see magic like this many years ago in Touba in Senegal when he was a boy."

Mouche could understand this, for she herself came from a country where the supernatural was accepted.

She said, "Then you don't hate him, Golo?"

The Senegalese produced another Gaulois and lit it, and the match illuminated the cream of his eyeballs. He replied, "Black man not allowed to hate."

Mouche drew in her breath sharply. "Ah," she cried, "I hate him! Dear God, how I hate him!"

Golo's cigarette glowed momentarily and he sighed likewise. The noises of the city and the fair were stilled except for the occasional shattering protest of the mangy and hungry lion caged at the far end. He said, "It good sometimes to hate. But I think it better not to. Sometimes when you hate, you forget if you sing. . . ."

His guitar was by his side, and so softly that it was barely audible he plucked out the melody of a Breton lullaby and he hummed it softly. Goodness knows where he had picked it up during the long, rough years of his perpetual exile from the land of his birth, in what camp, prison, or country he had heard it sung by another lonely expatriate from the hard-rocked, sea-fringed shores of Brittany. He remembered the words after a moment or two:

"My young one, my sweeting . . .
  Rock in your cradle . . .
 The sea rocks your father,
  The sea rocks his cradle,
 God grant you sweet sleep . . .
  God grant him return . . ."

When he played it again, Mouche began to sing it with him, rocking the two dolls in her arms, for that night she was more than half mad from what had been done to her.

Yet Golo had been right; the music worked its magic and

the hatred seemed to fade. In its place there returned an echo of that odd compassion she had so often felt for this evil man and which she had never understood.

Golo's eyes were closed and he was singing, dreaming and swaying:

"The storm winds are blowing,
  God rules the storm winds,
 Love God, my sweeting,
  Safe rides your father,
 God rocks his cradle,
  God sends you sleep . . ."

They sang it together in comfort and, not long after, in happiness. Golo left off playing. When the vibrations of the strings died away, Mouche went to sleep, the heads of Carrot Top and Mr. Reynardo still cradled to her breasts. The cigarette glowed yet a while longer and then was extinguished. Darkness and quiet fell over the Citroën and its strangely assorted inhabitants.

Inextinguishable was the hatred that Capitaine Coq felt for the drab he had taken to his bed, and soon he pushed her from the room and lay there cursing helplessly, what or why he did not know, except it was the thought of Mouche, her simplicity, her gentleness, her inviolability, and the impossibility of reducing her to the state of the woman he had just flung from his bed.

Yet the next day life returned once more to Carrot Top and Mr. Reynardo and all the others. Mouche again appeared before the booth to look after, abet, and interpret them to the children, large and small, infant and adult, who came to look and listen.

The tour was continued, but with a change. Thereafter Capitaine Coq took a second room for Mouche when they stayed overnight, and avoided contact with her as much as possible.

There was yet another difference, but this was more gradual in developing when they worked their way down through Annecy and Grenoble, heading for the South of France as the weather began to turn crisp and chill. The nature of the performance was changing.

More and more the stereotyped plot was abandoned, and the characters and the story wandered off into flights of imagination stemming from the schemes of Mr. Reynardo, the streak of poetry and imagination in Carrot Top, and Mouche's unique ability to enter into their make-believe instantly.

If they remained in a town for a week, a trip to the moon organized by Carrot Top with Dr. Duclos as scientific director might occupy them during the entire stay, with the result that people came back again and again to see how the affair was progressing, whether Gigi and Madame Muscat had succeeded in getting themselves taken along, and how Mouche was making out with Mr. Reynardo, who had a dishonest scheme for merchandising pieces of the moon as souvenirs.

Again the troupe appealed even more intimately to small communities where it played, by means of local gossip which seemed to collect astonishingly in the vicinity of the puppet booth, to the end that Carrot Top might call conspiratorially:

"Psst—Mouche—Reynardo. Come here. But don't tell the girls. I know a secret. . . ."

Mouche would move in closer, her plain face illuminated with excitement. "A secret. I love secrets. Oh, Carrots, tell me at once and I won't pass it on to a soul. . . ."

With his bogus smile Reynardo would insinuate, "Is there anything in it? Don't be a fool, Carrots. Tell me, maybe we can sell it——"

Carrots would protest, "'Oh, Rey, it isn't *that* kind of a secret. It won't keep forever. In fact, it won't keep much longer. I understand that Renée Duval, the wife of Carpenter Duval back there in the audience, is expecting a little addition. . . ."

Reynardo would yap, "What? Why, they were only just married. Wait—let me count. . . ." And lifting one paw, he would pretend to tick off the months, "September, October, November . . ." until Mouche would go over and stop him with "Reynardo—you mustn't. That's none of your business."

Then for the next few minutes, while the audience roared,

they would discuss the sex of the expected one; Dr. Duclos learnedly and stuffily discussed biology, Madame Muscat gave advice, Ali offered himself as baby sitter. Through the magic of Mouche's personality the villagers were swept into the middle of these odd doings and made a part of them.

Mouche was particularly adept at singling out wide-eyed children in the audience and summoning them over to meet the members of the cast, to shake hands with Ali to prove how harmless he was, stroke Mr. Reynardo, and converse with Carrot Top. They were unique, and the parts of France through which they made their way were not long in discovering it. The reputation of the talking and singing puppets and the live girl who stood out front and conversed with them was beginning to precede them, and when they reached Nice on the Côte d'Azur it had an effect that was to be far-reaching upon all of them.

Part Three

Moving south, they remained for ten days in Lyon for the big October Fair, pressed on to Marseille and Toulon, then ventured to rim the Côte d'Azur, the strip along the

Mediterranean devoted to the wealthy, and in Nice joined up with a large circus playing in a vacant lot not far from the seashore. They set up on the Midway as part of the side shows. The rich came slumming from the big hotels, paused momentarily by the booth, and were unable to tear themselves away.

The morning of the final day of the circus, which was then going on to Monte Carlo, a fat, untidy-looking old gentleman with a veined nose, the calculating eyes of a pig, and wearing a bowler hat and carrying a gold-headed cane, bustled up to Golo at the booth and demanded to see the proprietor.

The family was having its morning breakfast-get-together meeting before the day's performances began, which counted as a kind of warm-up during which plans for the day were discussed.

The old gentleman was immediately greeted by Carrot Top's shrill "Did you have an appointment?" and Reynardo's yapping laugh—"First he's got to have an appointment to make an appointment. That's my department. Who did you say you thought you were?"

Gigi bobbed up and sniggered unpleasantly. "Oh, I thought maybe it was somebody handsome."

Madame Muscat took her turn and reprimanded her. "Don't be a fool, Gigi. He's sure to be wealthy. Look at the fat on him. You don't get all that lard on your bones when there is a hole in your pocket."

It was obvious that the old fellow wasn't making a very good impression on the troupe, and Mouche apologized for them politely. "They're being very naughty today. You must forgive them. Perhaps I can help you."

It then turned out that he was an agent named Bosquet who booked acts for the Théâtre des Variétés in Nice and he wished to negotiate for the troupe to appear on the stage in the show as one of the turns.

The news threw the entire collection of puppets into a kind of frenzy of excitement, joy, worry, advice and counter-advice, plans and questions, with Mr. Reynardo yapping hysterically and thumping back and forth across the counter, shouting, "I'm going to be an actor. At last my true worth has been recognized. Ha, ha, it was me gave you the idea, wasn't it, Bosquet, old boy? Mouche, did you hear? We're all going on the stage. I want to play Cyrano. I've got just the nose for it. . . ."

It was a somewhat harrowing experience for Monsieur Bosquet, who was made to show his credentials by Dr. Duclos and submit to an interview conducted by Madame Muscat on the state of the morals of the theater, and then deal with Monsieur Nicholas and Carrot Top, so that in the end he became confused into paying more for the act than he had intended.

He never did get to see Capitaine Coq, for when the contract was completed Carrot Top took it below and returned with the document signed. Monsieur Bosquet then tried to make up for this by inviting Mouche to dine with him, for her thin, somewhat ungainly form, wide mouth, and luscious eyes beneath the dark hair suddenly stirred him.

He was routed in confusion when Mr. Reynardo appeared, leaning on one elbow and regarding him sardonically as he grated, "Why, you dirty, dirty old man. At your age! Aren't you ashamed of yourself, going after a baby, you with all those hairs growing out of your ears? I know what you're after."

On the other side of the stage Madame Muscat, with her arms akimbo, snorted, "I suspected you from the first. I said so to Dr. Duclos. What are you prepared to give her if she goes with you—diamonds, furs, a car, perhaps, hein? Not you, you old skinflint. . . . Don't listen to him, my dear. I know the kind. . . ."

Monsieur Bosquet fled while Reynardo roared with laughter.

The three weeks they took to prepare their act for the variety stage were not happy ones for Mouche, for while the rehearsals were as usual conducted by Carrot Top and Dr. Duclos, the sudden rise in the fortunes of the troupe seemed to have made Capitaine Coq more bitter and violent than ever. Aware that their engagement was due only to the catalytic presence of Mouche, he felt compelled to resent more than ever the fact that he owed to her an affluence and position he had never known before.

For some reason he had decided to abandon their successful formula and return to the puppet play they had given in the early days, and even the puppets appeared listless and seemed to respond mechanically to something in which they had long ago lost interest.

And so he was always at Mouche when they were together afterward, for her speech, her appearance, her country origins, endlessly reminding her, "I picked you up out of the gutter. When will you learn something better?" He criticized her walk, her clothes, her voice. It seemed as though he was almost determined to make their debut on the stage a failure.

But if so he was doomed to disappointment and had forgotten the strange independent will of the seven dolls and the electric relationship that existed between them and the girl.

For the first performance on any stage of Capitaine Coq and his family opened riotously on a Saturday evening to a packed house as with the first appearance of Mouche the puppets individually and collectively threw away the script, so to speak, and for twenty minutes furnished the audience with entertainment that verged from the hilarious, when Mr. Reynardo attempted to make himself up as Cyrano, to the touching, when Alifanfaron suffered an attack of stage fright.

They were presented against a set of a village square, with

Golo strumming his guitar to attract a crowd, but with the first appearance of Carrot Top and his excitement and delight at discovering the audience and his shrill shouts for Mouche to come and see, all pretense of giving an orderly show was abandoned and everyone, including Mouche, did exactly as he pleased.

Coq had originally provided a vulgar costume for Mouche. She came on instead in a simple skirt and peasant blouse, as natural as she was, her short-cut black hair and huge eyes shining in the spotlights that picked out the booth.

The puppets illuminated the theater with their excitement at being on a stage. They brought on embarrassed stage hands and electricians, whom Mouche at once put at ease; they attempted horribly garbled snatches from French classics; they made Mouche describe the members of the orchestra, whom they could not see; they demanded different-colored spotlights; they upset all tradition in a dozen different ways.

And as usual, Mouche forgot where she was and even who, and became the innocent and marveling playmate of the seven, and so carried them all straight to the hearts of the audience.

But while laughter ruled, the highlight was touched perhaps when Alifanfaron, at the first sight of so large an audience, froze into such a ludicrous and stammering attack of stage fright that not even Mouche could coax him out of it!

Golo strolled on out of the wings, plucking at his guitar. He chuckled and said in his soft, rich, African French, "Sometime when you scared, it helps if you sing your scare away."

His fingers created the notes he had once played for Mouche on a certain night long ago in far-off Besançon. The girl picked up the thread at once. She went to the big, stupid giant trembling and cowering in the booth and put her arm about him and, rocking him gently, sang with Golo:

"My young one, my sweeting . . .
   Rock in your cradle . . .
 The sea rocks your father . . ."

Carrot Top came up and joined in the chorus, and at the end the giant lifted his shaggy head, gazed out to all quarters of the audience, and announced ineffably, "I'm not scared any more." Carrot Top bounced over and patted Golo's cheek and kissed Mouche. The house was as hushed as though it were a church. Many in the audience were crying.

The next moment Mouche and Reynardo were romping through their own version of "Va t'en," with Gigi, the eternal soubrette, and later Madame Muscat and Dr. Duclos.

In the wings, during the performance, there stood a young man in blue tights with gold spangles and an overcoat thrown over his shoulders. Never once did he take his large, moist, handsome brown eyes from the face and figure of the girl by the puppet booth.

His name was Balotte, and he was an acrobat, a member of a troupe waiting to go onto the high trapeze in the turn that followed the puppet number. Other artists were likewise gathered there to watch the new act and found themselves as captivated as the audience.

But Balotte, who was a good, simple boy of somewhat limited intelligence and overweening vanity, was for the first time in his life falling in love with someone other than himself.

Looking out onto the stage at this gentle, gay, sincere, and motherly girl, he felt his heart touched as it had never been before. Yet at the same time he was filled with a professional's excitement at the show she was giving, for he appreciated what a girl who could make an audience sit up and take notice like that could do for him. He had long had it in his mind to go as a single and had been looking for a girl partner to throw him the handkerchief and stand about while he performed his feats.

The act came to a close to ear-shattering applause. Wave after wave of it poured over Mouche. She brought on each of the puppets for a bow. When the curtain closed upon her for the last time, she was standing with her back to the booth. Carrot Top had his cheek pressed against one of hers, an arm about her neck, Mr. Reynardo the other. Her eyes were shining. She had never been so happy.

When she came off, Balotte went to her and said, "Hola, little one. That was not bad, and I have seen many acts. Now stay here and watch me too. Afterward I will have something to say to you."

And so, out of politeness, Mouche remained in the wings and looked upward at the handsome boy as he swung, leaped, whirled, and somersaulted with his partners and occasionally threw her a look as he sat resting on the trapeze high up in the flies or brushed his mustache self-consciously.

Capitaine Coq came by, clad in black corduroy trousers and black high-necked sweater emphasizing his pallor, his fox-colored hair, and the cold glitter of his eyes. It was a commentary on his art that, outside of the stage manager, hardly anyone knew who he was. He paused for a moment and followed Mouche's glance upward. "Kinkers," he sneered, using the showman's derogatory term for acrobats, and spat. Then without another glance at Mouche he went on. He had made a date with a girl who played the flute in the orchestra. Now that he was becoming a success, it was time, he thought, to try it on with someone with a little class.

But Balotte, when he came sliding down the rope, was pleased, though not surprised, that Mouche had remained there watching him and said, "Well? All right, little one?"

Mouche replied sincerely, "'Oh yes, indeed. I thought you were wonderful."

"Oh, that wasn't anything. Wait until you see the new routine I am working up. Something really sensational."

"But isn't it fearfully dangerous?" Mouche asked. "Without a net or anything?"

Balotte preened himself. "But of course. That is what the public likes. See here, what about coming out with me for something to eat and a glass of beer?"

He was amazed at the expression of panic that crossed Mouche's face. "I . . . I don't know whether I can. I've never been before . . ."

Balotte came quickly to the point. "Is he your husband, that one? The fellow who calls himself Capitaine Coq?" he asked.

Mouche shook her head quickly. "Oh no. He is not."

Balotte was intelligent enough not to inquire any further. "Well, then, put on your street clothes and I'll meet you inside the stage door as soon as I have changed."

It was several minutes before Mouche could bring herself to believe that she was free to accept such an invitation. The bondage in which Capitaine Coq held her had become almost a habit, but even more, she belonged to the seven dolls and felt as though she should have asked Carrot Top for permission.

She hurried then to keep the rendezvous but found herself wishing she might have discussed with Madame Muscat the propriety of going out with a young man who had just introduced himself to her.

Balotte arrived shortly, hair sleeked down, the inevitable acrobat's white silk scarf around his neck and inside his jacket, and smelling faintly of perspiration mingled with liniment.

He was delighted by his success and flashed magnificent white teeth at her. Also, he took her most solicitously by the arm to guide her, as though she were fragile. It had been so long since a man had been gentle with her that it quite warmed Mouche's heart. All of a sudden she remembered that she was a young girl and laughed happily and, leaning on the sturdy arm of the young man, asked, "Where shall we go?"

They went to a water-front café at the far end of the Quai du Midi.

There, sitting out under the stars, they supped on highly seasoned bouillabaisse, which called for quantities of beer, which in turn made them lightheaded and merry.

They danced together, and contact with this stange girl made Balotte quite ardent and he held her close, but yet tenderly. The tenderness found an answering response in Mouche. Youth was wooing youth. For the first time in longer than she could remember, Mouche was enjoying herself in a normal manner. She felt as though she could never have enough of this magic night.

Everything was heightened, the sparkle of her eyes, the glitter of the stars, the swing of the music, the movement of her limbs, and of course the good looks of Balotte and the impression he was making.

Indeed, she was almost insatiable for innocent pleasure and did not wish to go home. Balotte, certain that it was his person and enthralling tales about his triumphs in the circus and variety world and his plans for future successes that made her so happy and gay, humored her, for he was enjoying himself too. When at four in the morning the café finally closed, they were the last to leave.

Balotte, for all his vanity, came of a good circus family and therefore, in love as he felt himself to be with Mouche, was respectful of her and honorable in his attentions toward another in his own profession. He took her home on a tram and left her at the door of her hotel with no more than a warm pressure of the hand and a loving look from his dark, liquid eyes.

When Mouche went inside she found Capitaine Coq waiting for her. He was slumped in a chair in the dingy, ill-smelling lobby, a cigarette hanging from his lip, but he was sober. The flute player had proved flabby, damp, self-accusing, and had drenched him with tears. His temper was even more vile than usual and he took it out on Mouche.

He said, "Come over here. Where the devil have you been? You'll be getting a regular salary now. You don't have to go out whoring in the streets."

Mouche felt hatred of this man so intensely that she thought she would become ill or faint. Yet the small taste of freedom she had enjoyed, the echoes of the innocent evening enabled her to face him. She replied, "I was out with Balotte. He asked me to have supper with him."

Coq laughed harshly. "Until four in the morning? That kind of dining we know. . . ."

"It is not true. We were dancing. Why shouldn't I dance with him? He is kind to me."

Capitaine Coq got up out of his chair, his hands and face working with rage. He ground his teeth and took her by the wrist so that she cried out with pain.

"That, and more of it," he shouted at her, applying more pressure. "If ever I catch you with that walking sweat gland again, I'll smash every bone in your body and in his too. Remember. Now get up to your room."

At the performance the next day Dr. Duclos, of all people, came up with a present for Mouche. It appeared he had been shopping and, passing a perfume counter, had so far abandoned caution as to invest in a small flacon. Oddly, it was the first perfume Mouche had ever had. They made her open it and try it on; Gigi jealously sampled some, Madame Muscat sniffed disdainfully, Ali tried to drink it because if it smelled so good it must taste better. For twenty minutes they elaborated this slender theme to the enchantment of the audience and ended with Mr. Reynardo in Mouche's arms, quite overcome and swooning.

As Mouche came off stage, Balotte, waiting to go on, whispered, "Tonight again?"

Mouche looked about her in alarm. "I don't dare. He has threatened to do you an injury."

Balotte snorted, "Ho! I can take care of myself. I know of a place where the music is even better. Be at the stage door again the same time, little one, eh?"

Mouche replied, "I don't know."

But she was there, hoping that Coq would not be about. She longed so for the gaiety and the sweet ease of being with someone who was kind. She did not have to wait. Balotte was there. And Capitaine Coq stepped out of a shadowed corner.

Capitaine Coq said, "Well, I can see that you both are asking for it. Have it then!" He whipped the backs of five bony fingers across Mouche's face, knocking her up against the wall. "Gutter slut!" he bawled at her.

Balotte made a menacing movement. Coq turned on him. "As for you, you muscle-headed kinker, you can hang by your tail like a monkey, but you wouldn't lift a finger for her or anybody else. I'm going to teach you to keep away from her."

But Capitaine Coq was wrong. Balotte was no coward, and furthermore, he had a body like iron, wrists of steel, and more than a little knowledge of the science of attack and defense.

The fight was short and savage, both men moiling, writhing, and striking in silence with no sound but the whistling of their breathing, the thud of blows, and the grunts of pain. Then it was over, with Capitaine Coq lying in a battered, bloodied heap upon the floor, stunned, whipped, and unable to rise. He was bleeding from the nose and mouth and a gash in his cheek, and one eye was closing.

With his red hair, crinkled pale face and black suit, he was the personification of the devil dethroned, evil conquered by good, as the young acrobat stood over him, panting but unmarked. He was the villain foiled, the wicked bully who at last receives his just deserts. He lay in an untidy heap like a horrid insect that has been squashed.

Mouche stood by the wall, her hand to her own bruised lips, staring down at him. So had she prayed to see him, beaten, cowed, mastered. Yet she was conscious only of being filled with sadness and of an ache in her throat comparable to that experienced sometimes before the puppet booth when one or the other of its inhabitants was particularly moving. She had not known that a wish fulfilled could be so empty and that the physical destruction of the object of her hatred would yield no more than the desire to weep for the downfall of evil.

Balotte moved over to him, prepared to kick him unconscious if need be, and asked, "Want any more?"

The glassy eyes of Capitaine Coq filled with venom, but he

shook his head, mumbling something unintelligible, and did not attempt to get up.

Balotte said, "Come along then, Mouche. This fellow won't give you any more trouble."

They went out then arm in arm and Mouche did not look back at the heap on the floor, for had she done so, she could not have gone. This time they did not dance, as if by mutual understanding they recognized it was not the time, but instead sat in a corner booth, eating and getting acquainted. And under the stimulus of the youth and wooing of Balotte, Mouche's mood of sorrow evaporated. They walked home and stood for a while by the promenade, looking out over the harbor with Nice's necklace of lights curving away from them and the stars cascading over the black, frowning wall of the mountains behind the city. Balotte kissed her, and gratefully Mouche returned his kisses.

At the next performance of Capitaine Coq and His Family, Carrot Top appeared with a black eye and was raucously greeted by Mr. Reynardo and the rest of the cast demanding to know how it had happened, with Carrot Top insisting that he had walked into a door in the dark. They devoted the act to discussing the truth of this plus the best remedies, Madame Muscat finally arriving with a small piece of *filet* which Mouche solicitously bound to the optic. All through the show she felt herself unaccountably close to tears. Yet she was glad for the pressure of Balotte's hand as he passed her and whispered, "Petite Mouche, tonight we dance."

This was the night, too, that the manager of the theater stood at the door and counted more than two hundred patrons who had been there the week before and who had returned to see what mischief the family of Capitaine Coq were up to.

As the second month of the engagement drew to a close and it was obvious that the puppet show was as popular as ever and a decided drawing card, the management decided to retain them but change the rest of the bill. This meant that, among others, the company of aerialists of which Balotte was a member would be moving on.

One night, therefore, a little more than a week before this was to take place, as they sat on their favorite bench on the sea promenade and watched the moon set, Balotte asked Mouche to marry him and was accepted.

"You will see," he had said. "As my assistant in my new act, you will make me famous, and yourself too. We will tour the world together."

But also he had told her that he loved her.

Mouche responded to his sincerity and his gentleness. She had been happy during those weeks that Balotte had been courting her. Against the normality of their relationship and his simplicity, the walks they took together, the picnic lunches in the hills, the nightmare of her relationship to Capitaine Coq could be recognized and Mouche knew that an end must be made to it. She was sure that she loved Balotte, for he was handsome, kind, and sympathetic to her and there was no reason why she should not.

It had been a particularly trying week for Mouche, for although since the beating Coq had offered her no further violence or tried to interfere with her dates with Balotte, he was bitter and sneering and his tongue had never been nastier as he took her to task before stage hands and performers. His movements became more and more mysterious. Sometimes she would not see him for a whole day. Then the next he seemed always at her elbow, biting, mocking, sardonic, or abusive.

It was said that he would spend long hours sitting in the puppet booth in silence, and once the night watchman, making his rounds in the theater between the hours of midnight and eight, when the scrubwomen came, swore that he heard the voices of the puppets coming from the booth in some kind of argument, but by the time he made his way from the balcony to the stage there seemed to be no one there, and only the empty gloves of the Reynardo and Gigi puppets were found lying on the counter of the booth.

Capitaine Coq received the news of Mouche's forthcoming marriage and departure from the show with surprising calmness. Perhaps he had been expecting it. They went to him together, for Mouche had not the courage to face him alone. She declared her intention of remaining with the show until the end of the month, when the contract expired. Then she and Balotte would be married and she would leave.

He had listened to her with a curious expression on his cynical countenance and then had simply shrugged and turned away, vanishing in the direction of his dressing room, which was on the other side of the stage from that occupied by Mouche. And thereafter for the remainder of the engagement she never saw him again.

But if Coq appeared to accept Mouche's decision to marry Balotte and leave the act, with a certain amount of resignation, the seven little creatures whom Mouche met twice daily in the pool of spotlights focused on the shabby little puppet booth on-stage took the event over, discussed it and harped on it endlessly.

Each reacted according to his or her nature to Mouche's romance and engagement, and Madame Muscat's attempts to ascertain whether Mouche knew the facts of life and her advice to her for her wedding night were one of the most hilarious evenings the old theater had ever known.

Day after day Mouche went through some kind of catechism with regard to her plans and her future. Where would she go? Where would she live? Where was she going to be married? Gigi wanted to know about her trousseau, and Dr. Duclos gave a pompous pseudo-scientific lecture on genetics and just why her children were likely to be acrobats. Mr. Reynardo tried to get the catering job for the wedding and Alifanfaron applied for the job of nurse.

Yet to anyone witnessing one or more of these performances, it became evident that for all of the childish interest and seeming lighthearted banter, the fact of Mouche's approaching marriage and departure hung over them, filled with the tragic implications of children about to lose the security of the presence of one who was both loved and loving.

Through every show there ran a vein of dread of the day, a forlornness, a helplessness, and a dumb pleading that wrung Mouche's heart, for with her departure becoming imminent she herself did not know how she would be able to leave these little people who in the past year had become such a part of her and the only real friends, companions, and playmates she had ever known.

Often, while Mouche would be in conversation with one character, another would appear from below, retire to the end of the booth, stare silently and longingly at her, then heave a large sigh and vanish again. The pressure upon Mouche was becoming intolerable and she did not know how she would be able to reach the final night without breaking, for Balotte could not help her. He was pleased with the publicity that had come his way and the applause that greeted his appearances now that he was the bridegroom-to-be of a romantic story that had been written up in the newspapers. He had no idea of what was happening to Mouche.

The final performance of Capitaine Coq and His Family, which took place in the Théâtre des Variétés on the Saturday night of December 15, was one that Mouche would not forget as long as she lived.

The old theater with its red velvet drapes, gold-encrusted boxes, and shimmering candelabra had been sold out for more than a week. Word had spread along the Côte d'Azur, and there were visitors from Cannes, St. Tropez, Antibes, and Monaco. Half of the audience present were regulars who had fallen in love over the weeks with Mouche or the seven dolls and who had paid premiums to be there. The front rows sparkled with jewels and décolletage and white shirt fronts. The playboys and playgirls of the gold coast had a wonderful nose for the unusual, and slightly amer, the bitter-sweet in entertainment, the story behind the story, the broken heart palpitating on-stage for all to see. The gossip had gone around the cocktail circuit, "My dear, it's frightfully amusing. She talks with all these little dolls, but there's supposed to be the most fantastic man behind them. No one has ever seen him. He's supposed to be madly in love with her. Philippe has four tickets. We're all driving over and dining at the Casino first."

It began as usual with the strains of "Va t'en, va t'en" dying away in the orchestra pit, followed by curtain rise showing a corner of the village square with the puppet booth set up and Golo, the white patch gleaming over his vacant eye socket, strumming his guitar in front of it in a little song dedicated to calling the village folk together to see their show.

The spotlight on Golo would dim; the light pools by the booth would narrow. One of the puppets would appear with startling suddenness in the limelight and claim the attention of all. Mouche was never on-stage as the curtain went up.

This night it began with Mr. Reynardo making a furtive appearance on the counter of the booth, looking carefully to the right and left and behind him as well. Then he called: "Pssssst! Golo!" And when Golo appeared from behind the booth: "Where's Mouche?"

"I don't know, Mr. Reynardo. You want me to call her?"

"In a minute. I've got something for her." He ducked down and appeared with a handsome red fox fur scarf tipped with a bushy tail at one end and a small fox mask at the other. He stretched it along the counter and for a moment snuffled up and down its length. "It's for her," he told Golo.

"*Dieu!*" remarked Golo. "But that's rich. I'll go fetch Mouche, Mr. Reynardo."

While Golo went off into the wings, Mr. Reynardo scrutinized the scarf closely. "Eeeeeh!" he said with some slight distaste. "Awfully familiar. Say, she was a nice-looking babe. . . . I seem to remember her from somewhere." He moved up to

98

the head of the scarf and bestowed a surprisingly gentle kiss onto the muzzle of the fox mask. "*Requiescat in pace*, kid," he said, "and keep Mouche warm."

Mouche walked on-stage into a storm of applause that lasted for several minutes and brought the ache back to her throat. Whenever she was shown kindness or approval it brought her close to tears.

At last she was able to proceed. She began, "Golo said you were looking for me, Rey . . ."

"Uh-huh. Glad you got here before the others. Er . . . ah . . ." The fox was looking not entirely comfortable. He reached and, taking the scarf in his jaws, he held it out to the girl. "This is for you. It's a wed——" He seemed to gag over the words and switched: ". . . a going-away present for you."

Mouche's hand flew to her heart. "Oh, Rey! How beautiful. Oh, you shouldn't have . . . You know you shouldn't have spent so much . . ."

Her expression altered suddenly to the wise, tender, and slightly admonishing "Mother-knows-all-what-have-you-done-now" look that her audiences knew so well. "Rey! Come over here to me at once and tell me where you got that beautiful and expensive scarf."

The fox squirmed slightly. "Must I, Mouche?"

"Reynardo! You know what I have always told you about being honest. . . ."

By a twist of his neck Mr. Reynardo managed to achieve a look of injured innocence. "Well, if you must know, I bought it on the hire-purchase installment plan."

"Indeed. And what happens if you fail to keep up the payments? Oh, Rey! I suppose they'll come to my home and take it away from me."

The fox slowly shook his head. "Oh, now . . . You see, I made a kind of a deal."

Mouche was mock serious now and once more lost in their make-believe. She knew the kind of sharp practice to which he was prone. She asked, "And pray, what kind of a deal, Mr. Reynardo?"

"We-e-e-ll . . . If I fail to keep up the installments the man gets something else in exchange. I signed a paper. It's all settled."

Mouche walked right into the trap. "Did you? And just what is he to have in exchange for this exquisite fur piece?"

The fox appeared to swallow once, then modestly turned his head aside before he replied meekly, "Me."

Struck to the heart, Mouche cried, "Oh, my dear—— You mean you've pawned yourself—— Oh, Rey . . . I don't know what to say. . . ."

For a moment Mouche glanced out across the footlights, and the balcony spot picked up two drops of light traversing her cheeks and splintered them so that they glowed like diamonds.

Like a flash the fox was across the stage of the booth and whipped his red, furry head with the black mask and long nose into the hollow of Mouche's shoulder and snuggled there with a contented sigh in the manner of a naughty child that takes immediate advantage of any tenderness.

The contact came close to breaking Mouche's heart for love of this sly, wicked little creature whose mischief and amorality stemmed from the fact that it was his nature and he did not know any better. Yet he tried hard to please her and be honest for her sake.

Thereafter the other puppets appeared to delight and torture Mouche still further with their parting gifts and little made-up awkwardly sincere speeches.

Dr. Duclos presented her with an encyclopedia. "Everything I know is inside this book," the formally dressed penguin pontificated. "Thought you might like to have it handy for information on all subjects when I am not around any longer."

Gigi gave her a trousseau negligee and nightgown set and a grudging kiss, while Madame Muscat handed her a rolling pin and an egg beater, remarking significantly, "A marriage can be kept in order with these, my dear. And remember, all men are beasts, but necessary ones." From Alifanfaron she received a photograph of himself, and Monsieur Nicholas gave her an oddly turned piece of wood that was not one but many shapes.

"For your first-born," he said. "It is a toy I have made for him that is not any, yet is still all toys, for in his imagination, when he plays with it, it will be whatever he sees in it or wishes it to be."

Golo came forward. He had a little African good-luck god he had carved for her out of a piece of ebon wood. Like the white-shafted spotlights beamed down from above, the emotions and tensions of everyone in the theater seemed concentrated on this one spot, the shabby little booth, the Negro with the gleaming patch over one eye who was crying unashamedly, and the girl who was trying desperately to hold herself together.

From where she was standing, Mouche could look into the wings and see the show girls, singers, dancers, acrobats, and stage hands gathered there, watching and listening, as spell-bound as the audience. She saw Balotte in his blue spangled tights, his beautiful body proud and erect, and he looked like a stranger to her.

Carrot Top appeared alone contriving to look more worried and forlorn than usual. He was empty-handed. He tried to appear nonchalant by whistling, but it soon petered out when his lips seemed to have trouble pursing themselves for the whistle. Finally he gave it up, saying, "Oh, what's the use? I'm not fooling anybody. I came to say good-by, Mouche."

Mouche said, "Good-by, dear Carrot Top."

"Will you miss me?"

"Oh yes, Carrot Top. I shall miss you terribly."

"Shall you be having children of your own, Mouche?"

"Yes . . ."

"Will they be like us?"

"Oh I hope so. . . . I do hope so. . . ."

Carrot Top was silent a moment and then said, "I didn't get you anything. I couldn't. I'll give you my love to take with you, Mouche. . . ."

Now the ache was closing her throat again. "Carrot Top! Do you really love me?" In all the time they had been together, he had never once said it.

The puppet nodded. "Oh yes. I always have. Only you never noticed. Never mind. It's too late now. Mouche, will you give me a going-away present?"

"Oh yes, Carrots. Anything I have."

"Will you sing a song with me?"

"Of course, Carrots. What shall it be?"

The little doll said, "Golo knows."

The Senegalese appeared and picked out an introduction on his guitar. It was the Breton lullaby. Mouche had not expected this. She did not know whether she could get through it.

Carrot Top held out his hand to her and she took it in both of hers. They sang:

"My young one, my sweeting . . .
  Rock in your cradle . . .

The storm winds are blowing,
  God rules the storm winds . . ."

When they had finished, Golo wandered away quietly into
the wings and Carrot Top reached up and kissed Mouche's
cheek.

"Don't forget us when you have children of your own,
Mouche." He vanished beneath the counter.

The others came whipping up by twos to cry, "Don't forget
us, Mouche," and overwhelm her with pecks and kisses.

Mouche, her eyes now blinded by tears, opened her arms and
cried to them as though there was no one else there but them
and her, "Oh no, no! I can never forget you. My darlings, I
will never forget you. You will always be like my own children
and as dear to me——"

She hardly heard the band swing into its closing theme, or
the heavy swish of the descending curtains, closing them out
from the tempest of applause and cheers from the audience out
front. The last thing that Mouche saw and heard was Mr.
Reynardo, his muzzle turned skyward, howling like a coyote,
and Alifanfaron with his head buried in the folds of the side
curtains of the puppet booth.

Then she fled to her dressing room, locked the door, and,
putting her head down on her arms, wept. Nor could she be
persuaded by knocks or shouts from without to open the door

and emerge to take her bows. She felt as though she would cry endlessly for the rest of her life.

She would not open even when Balotte came to fetch her, and begged him to go, promising to meet him at his hotel in the morning, and finally he too departed.

She remained sitting in the dark of her dressing room for a long while.

On every stage in the world at night after the performance is over, there stands a single, naked electric light bulb. No spot seems as glaring as where the incandescent sheds its halo, no shadows as long and deep and grotesque as those lurking at the bulb's extreme range, spilling over flats and props, pieces of sets and furniture.

Against the brick rear wall of the theater, almost at the farthest edge of the illumination, yet visible, stood the deserted puppet booth, its white oilcloth sign, "Capitaine Coq et Sa Famille," barely legible.

Unseen in the shadows, squatting on his haunches, Golo sorrowed alone in the dark in the manner of his people. It was nearly four o'clock in the morning, and the theater was empty.

Mouche slipped from her dressing room for the last time. She carried a small dressing case in which she had packed her few personal belongings. Her wardrobe she was leaving behind her, just as she was leaving a part of herself behind, the Mouche that had been and would never be again.

To reach the stage door it was necessary for her to cross the dark, cavernous stage. From the passageway she stepped into the wings beyond the range of the single light that would have guided her across. And out of this darkness a hand reached and grasped her by the wrist and another was placed across her mouth before she could cry out with the fright that momentarily stopped her heart.

Had the distant light reflected upon the pale, hate-ravaged features and red hair of Capitaine Coq, Mouche's heart might never have started beating again.

But the hard calluses on the fingers covering her lips told their story, and a gleam of white eyeballs completed the identification.

Golo whispered into her ear, "For the love of the dear God, do not make a sound."

As quietly, Mouche asked against the pounding of her heart, "What is it, Golo?"

"I don't know. Something is happening. Stay here with me, Miss Mouche, but make no noise. Golo very much afraid."

He pulled her gently down to her knees beside him, and she could feel that he was trembling.

"But, Golo . . ."

"Shhhhh, Miss Mouche. Don't speak. Listen . . ."

At first there was no sound but their own soft breathing. Then there came a faint rustling and scratching. It appeared to come from somewhere near the center of the stage. Sight came to the aid of straining ears, and Golo pressed Mouche's hand hard with his as the head of Carrot Top rose slowly above the counter of the puppet booth and reconnoitered carefully.

There was something horrible in the caution with which he looked to the right and to the left, and then, with that extraordinarily lifelike movement with which he was endowed, leaned out from the ends of the booth and gazed behind as well; horrible, too, was the fact that no one was supposed to be there, that the performance was to an empty theater, or perhaps even more horrible still that it was no performance at all. . . .

Golo whispered, "He gone away early, but *they* came back. I knew they were here. I felt it."

It was Mouche's turn to quiet him, and she pressed his arm gently and said, "Shhhhhhhh."

Having made certain there was no one about, Carrot Top retired to the far end of the counter and let his face sink into his hands and remained thus for a minute or two.

Then the quiet was disturbed by a rasping, gravelly whisper: "That you up there, Carrots?"

The redheaded puppet slowly lifted his head from his hands, looked down deliberately, and replied, "Yes."

"Is the coast clear?"

"Yes. There's nobody here."

"Where's the watchman?"

"Asleep in the boiler room."

The head of the sharp-faced fox arose from below. He too reconnoitered for a moment, then, satisfied, leaned on the counter at the opposite end from Carrot Top. Finally the leprechaun said in a listless and woebegone voice, "Well, what do we do now?"

Reynardo sighed, then replied, "I don't know, if you don't. You've been running the show, Carrot Top. Kind of messed it up, didn't you, old fellow?"

Carrot Top reflected. "Did I? I suppose I did. I never thought she'd leave us for that knuckle-head. She'll never be happy with him."

"Why didn't you tip her off?"

"Madame Muscat tried, but it was no use. She's too young to see that monkey will never think of anyone but himself."

"Is she really going to marry him, Carrot Top?"

"Oh yes. It's all over."

The fox said, "*Merde!*"

Carrot Top reproved him. "Oh, cut it out, Rey. It won't help to use bad language. You know how *she* hated it. The thing is we've got to decide what to do. Is there any use in going on?"

Mr. Reynardo replied quickly, "Not as far as I'm concerned. She was the only thing I ever cared about. I'm ready to call it a day."

"Me too. I suppose we ought to put it to a vote."

"Uh-huh. Take the chair, Carrots. I'll call the roll. Ali?"

The voice of the giant came from below the counter. "I'm here, I think."

"Dr. Duclos?"

"Present."

"Gigi?"

"Yes."

"Madame Muscat?"

"Of course."

"Monsieur Nicholas?"

"Yes, yes."

Mr. Reynardo said, "All present and accounted for," and folded his arms.

Carrot Top then made a little speech in a not too firm voice. "Ladies and gentlemen of our company. Inasmuch as our well-loved sister Mouche has left us to be married and will never return, I have called this meeting to decide what is to be done. The question before the committee of the whole is: Shall we try to continue without her?"

Dr. Duclos commented, "What's the use if nobody comes to see us, Mr. Chairman?"

Reynardo turned it around: "What's the use if we can't see her?"

Gigi's voice remarked, "We could get someone like her to take her place."

Alifanfaron was heard to rumble: "Gee, I'm stupid, but even I know there's no one like her. Nobody could take her place."

Madame Muscat contributed, "Well, we had a show we used to do before she came to us."

The deep voice of Monsieur Nicholas sounded from below. "Do you wish to return to that? And sleeping in haystacks again? One can never go back. . . ."

Gigi's girlish treble inquired anxiously, "But if there isn't anything forward?"

"Then," replied Monsieur Nicholas, "perhaps the best idea is to go nowhere."

"Oh," exclaimed Carrot Top. "How?"

"Simply by ceasing to exist."

Carrot Top said "Oh" again and Reynardo rasped, "Ha-ha, suits me." While Dr. Duclos said pompously, "Logically sound, I must admit, however unpleasant the prospect." Ali complained, "I don't know what you're talking about. All I know is if I can't be with Mouche I want to die."

Mr. Reynardo sniggered, "That's the general idea, Ali, old boy. You've hit it for once. Put it to a vote, Mr. Chairman."

There was a moment of silence. Then Carrot Top said firmly, "All in favor of ceasing to exist say 'Aye.' "

There was a scattered chorus of "Ayes" and one squeaky "No" from Gigi.

Reynardo graveled: "Motion carried. Proceed, Mr. Chairman."

"Now?" Carrot Top asked. There were no dissents.

He continued: "Next question—how?"

Dr. Duclos said, "I have always been fascinated by self-immolation; the Indian custom of suttee, where the widow casts herself upon the funeral pyre of her deceased spouse."

Reynardo said, "I don't see the connection, but the idea isn't bad. Fire is clean."

Carrot Top said, "There's a vacant lot back of the theater."

Gigi suddenly wailed, "But I don't want to die."

Reynardo ducked down beneath the counter swiftly and came up with the half doll that was Gigi—empty, her eyes staring vacuously—clamped in his jaws. Then he carefully dropped her over the side of the booth onto the stage, where she fell with a small crash that echoed shockingly through the empty theater. "Then live, little golden-haired pig," he said.

Mouche drew in her breath and whispered, "Poor, poor little Gigi . . ."

Mr. Reynardo looked over the side of the booth at the little heap lying on the stage and then asked, "Anybody else want to back out?"

Madame Muscat pronounced Gigi's epitaph: "She was never much good anyway."

Alifanfaron said: "But she was so pretty."

Carrot Top sighed briefly. "One of the world's great illusions, the golden-haired fairy princess . . ."

"Who in the end turns out to be nothing more than a walking appetite," Reynardo concluded, for he had never liked Gigi much.

Monsieur Nicholas said from below: "It is not necessary to be unkind. God made her as she was, as He made us all."

Alifanfaron asked, "Gee, what will become of God when we are gone?"

The voice of Monsieur Nicholas replied after a moment of reflection: "I think perhaps God will destroy Himself too if it is indeed true that He has created us all in His own image. . . ."

Carrot Top asked, "Why?"

"Because if He is God He could not bear to contemplate such a miserable failure of His designs."

Mr. Reynardo stretched his neck and looked down below the counter. "Oh," he said. "That's clever of you. I hadn't thought about it in that way."

"Most profound," contributed Dr. Duclos, "not to mention praglatic——"

Carrot Top corrected him almost absent-mindedly, "Pragmatic." He sighed then and added, "Well, then, it's good-by to Capitaine Coq and His Family."

Golo turned a stricken face toward Mouche. "They going to die. Don't let them, Miss Mouche."

Mr. Reynardo went over to Carrot Top and stuck out his paw. "So long, kid. It wasn't a bad ride while it lasted."

Carrot Top took it and shook it solemnly. "Good-by, Rey. You've always been a friend. I'll go down and get things ready."

Mouche arose. Her knees were stiff from kneeling, her heart was pounding with excitement, and her throat was dry. She picked up her small valise and marched across the stage, her heels clicking on the boards and the single standing light picking up her slender shadow, speeding it ahead of her and throwing it as a kind of prophecy of her coming athwart the puppet booth and its single inhabitant.

It was astonishing, this repetition of the first time that Mouche had encountered the puppets of Capitaine Coq.

There was the same darkness with the single light to probe the shadows; there was the mysterious booth looming out of the shadows, the lone puppet perched on the counter, and the slender figure of a girl marching by carrying a valise.

Except now the show was on the other foot, and it was Mouche who paused in the spill of yellow light before the puppet booth and called to the small figure flattened on the counter there, "Hello, baby . . ."

Mr. Reynardo, the composed, the cynical, and the self-assured, was taken aback. His whole frame shuddered as he reared up and peered through the gloom, for he was handicapped by having to look directly into the light. His jaws moved silently several times and finally he managed to produce a croak.

"Mouche! Where have you been? Have you been around here long?"

Mouche paused before the booth and set her valise down. She contemplated the agitated and nonplused fox jittering back and forth. Finally she said, "Never mind where I have been. I know where you are going. There is nothing to be found in the heart of flames but the ashes of regret. I'm ashamed of you all."

The fox stopped flapping and contemplated her long and hard. "We didn't know you were here." Then he added, "We voted . . ."

"Was it a fair vote?" Mouche asked.

The fox swallowed. "Well, maybe Monsieur Nicholas, Carrot Top, and I rigged it a little. But it was only because of you —going away and leaving us, I mean."

"And Gigi here?" Mouche bent over and picked up the empty doll.

The fox looked uneasy. He flattened his head to the counter and thereby seemed to have moved his eyes guiltily. He said, "We pushed her out of the nest. We excommunicated her."

"We?"

"I did. She didn't love you. . . ."

"It was wrong, Rey."

He hung his head. "I know it. Don't leave us, Mouche."

"Rey—you're blackmailing me again like you always have—with love. . . ."

There might have been the well-dressed, attentive, cultured audience of the night before out front instead of the blank, staring empty seats; there might have been the rabble from the slums, washed up from the edge of the street fair, gathered about the booth; there might have been the peasant children and the village people gathered about them on the village square—it made no difference. When the puppets were there and she talking with them, she lost herself, she lost reality, she lost the world—there remained only these, her friends and companions and their need.

The hoarse voice of the fox dropped to a rattling whisper again. "This time it isn't blackmail, Mouche. If you must go, take me with you."

"And leave the others? Rey, you can't desert them now."

The wary figure of the fox stirred. He moved imperceptibly closer to where Mouche was standing. "Oh yes, I can. I don't care about anything or anybody. Let me come, Mouche. I'm housebroken. And you know me—gentle with children."

The old habits were so hard to break. Momentarily Mouche forgot about herself and that she had parted with all this, that this was the beginning of the morning that was to see her wedded to Balotte and a new and normal life. She went to the booth and, bending over in her sweetly tender and concerned manner, admonished, "But don't you see, Rey, that's being disloyal."

Mr. Reynardo appeared to ponder this for a moment. Then he moved closer and barely nuzzled the tip of his snout onto the back of Mouche's hand. He sighed deeply and said: "I know. But what's the dif? Everybody knows I'm a heel. They expect it of me. And to tell you the truth, it's a relief to be one again. I've tried to be a good fellow, but it doesn't work—not unless you're around to keep me from backsliding. . . ."

She could not help herself. She placed a caressing hand upon the bristly redhead. "My poor Rey . . ."

Instantly the fox whipped his head into the hollow between neck and shoulder and was whispering, "Mouche—take care of me. . . ."

The touch of him was as always an exquisitely tender agony. Her heart swelled with love for this unhappy creature. With startling suddenness Alifanfaron bobbed up.

"Oh gee, excuse me. Am I interrupting something? Goodness, it's Mouche. Are you back again, Mouche? If you're back again I don't want to die any more."

The fox grated: "Damn! Why did you have to come up just then? I nearly had her." He vanished.

Mouche said, "But, Ali dear, I cannot stay, I'm going to be

married, and I don't want you to die. . . . What shall I do?" They had all the deadly logical illogicality of children.

"Take me along, Mouche. You don't know what it is to be a giant and stupid and lose a friend. . . ."

Mouche had heard herself say, "I'm going to be married," but it was like something someone else said about another person. Where was that real world now, the world of sanity and things as they ought to be to which she had been fleeing to save herself from complete destruction? Now she could remember only how she had always felt about Alifanfaron's troubles.

"Oh, Ali," she cried, "you're not really stupid. It's just that you were born too big in a world filled with people who are too small."

"Ah hooom! Harrrumph! Exactly, my dear. A very trenchant remark. Most sage indeed." It was Dr. Duclos, the penguin, in formal attire as usual, his pince-nez attached to a black ribbon perched on the end of his beak. He peered at her for a moment and then said, "So glad to see you're back. We've all missed you frightfully." He went away.

Carrot Top appeared, whistling a snatch of "Va t'en, va t'en," and then with a simulated surprise discovered the girl standing at her accustomed place slightly to the right of the center of the booth. He said, "Oh, hello, Mouche. You still here?"

"I was just leaving. Carrot Top, come here . . ."

He edged tentatively a little closer, but was wary. Mouche said, "I overheard everything. I couldn't help it. Aren't you ashamed?"

Carrot Top said, "Oh," and was lost in thought for a moment. Then the small boy with the red hair, bulbous nose, pointed ears, and wistful, longing face said reflectively, "It was going to be quite queer without you. Oh yes, quite queer. At first I thought I might be able to go places again. You were always holding me down, you know."

"Oh, Carrot Top—dear little Carrots," Mouche said, "I never wanted to."

Carrot Top mused, "I wonder. You were always pointing out my duty to Gigi, for instance. And there was never anything behind that pretty face. At first, after you left, I thought I might be able to——"

"Yes, yes, I know—fly," Mouche concluded for him as the sudden tears filled her eyes, and for a moment she was unable to see the booth or Carrot Top. "Fly then, Little Carrots. No one will keep you back now. Reach for the stars and they will tumble into your lap."

The puppet emitted a mortal wail. "But I don't want to fly, really. I don't want the stars. I only want to be with you forever, Mouche. Take me with you." He slithered across the counter and rested his head on Mouche's breast, and beneath the pressure of the little figure she could feel the wild beating of her heart.

"Carrots—dear Carrots . . . I have always loved you."

The doll turned his head and looked her full in the face. "Do you? But you don't really love us, Mouche, not really, otherwise you couldn't go away."

A moan of pain almost animal in its intensity was torn from Mouche. She cried, "Oh, I do, I do. I love you all. I have loved you so much and with all my heart. It is only him I hate so terribly that there is room for nothing else, not even love any more."

Standing there in the darkness, lost as it were in the center of the vast universe of the empty stage, she could bring herself to speak the truth to a doll that she had never spoken to a human.

"I loved him. I loved him from the first moment I saw him. I loved him and would have denied him nothing. He took me and gave me only bitterness and evil in return for all I had for him, all the tenderness and love, all the gifts I had saved for him. My love turned to hate. And the more I hated him, the more I loved you all. Carrots . . . How long can such deep love and fearful hatred live side by side in one human being before the host goes mad? Carrots, Carrots— let me go. . . ."

Yet she put up her hands and pressed the head of Carrot Top

close to her neck, and suddenly Mr. Reynardo was there too, and the touch of the two little objects made her wish to weep endlessly and hopelessly. She closed her eyes, wondering if her mind would crack.

She was startled by the shrill voice of Carrot Top: "But who are we, Mouche?"

The remark was echoed by Mr. Reynardo, but when she opened her eyes the pair was gone and instead Monsieur Nicholas was regarding her from behind the panes of his square spectacles.

The little figure had the effect of calming her momentarily, for the old habits were still strong. Here was her reliable friend and philosopher and counselor who appeared inevitably in the booth when matters threatened to get out of hand, mender of broken toys and broken hearts.

Yet he too asked the question that brought her again close to panic. "Who are we all, my dear, Carrot Top and Mr. Reynardo, Alifanfaron and Gigi, Dr. Duclos and Madame Muscat, and even myself?"

Mouche began to tremble and held to the side of the booth lest she faint. Worlds were beginning to fall; defenses behind which she had thought to live in safety and blindness were crumbling.

Who were they indeed? And what had been the magic that had kept them separate, the seven who were so different, yet united in love and kindness, and the one who was so monstrous?

Monsieur Nicholas spoke again. "Think, Mouche. Whose hand was it you just took to you so lovingly when it was Carrot Top or Mr. Reynardo or Alifanfaron, and held it close to your breast and bestowed the mercy of tears upon it?"

Mouche suppressed a cry of terror. "The hand that struck me across the mouth . . ." she gasped, and her own fingers went to her lips as though in memory of that pain.

"Yet you loved it, Mouche. And those hands loved and caressed you——"

Mouche felt her senses beginning to swim, but now it was she who asked the question. "But who are you, then, Monsieur Nicholas? Who are you all?"

Monsieur Nicholas seemed to grow in stature, to fill the booth with his voice and presence as he replied, "A man is many things, Mouche. He may wish like Carrot Top to be a poet and soar to the stars and yet be earth-bound and overgrown, ugly and stupid like Alifanfaron. In him will be the seeds of jealousy, greed, and the insatiable appetite for admiration and pleasure of chicken-brained arrogant Gigi. Part of him will be a pompous bore like Dr. Duclos and another the counterpart of Madame Muscat, gossip, busybody, tattletale, and sage. And where there is a philosopher there can also be the sly, double-dealing sanctimonious hypocrite, thief, and self-forgiving scoundrel like Mr. Reynardo."

And Monsieur Nicholas continued, "The nature of man is a never-ending mystery, Mouche. There we are, Mouche, seven of us you have grown to love. And each of us has given you what there was of his or her heart. I think I even heard the wicked Reynardo offer to lay down his life for you—of his skin. He was trying to convey to you a message from Him who animates us all. . . ."

"No, no—— No more!" Mouche pleaded. "Stop. I cannot bear it."

"Evil cannot live without good," Monsieur Nicholas said in a voice that was suddenly unlike his own. "All of us would rather die than go on without you."

"Who is it? Who is speaking?" Mouche cried. And then on a powerful impulse, hardly knowing what she was doing, she reached across the booth to the curtain through which she could be seen but could not see, and with one motion stripped away the veil that for so long had separated her from the wretched, unhappy man hiding there.

He sat there immovable as a statue, gaunt, hollow-eyed, bitter, hard, uncompromising, yet dying of love for her.

The man in black with the red hair, in whose dead face only the eyes still lived, was revealed with his right hand held high, his fingers inside the glove that was Monsieur Nicholas. In his left was crumpled in a convulsive grip the limp puppet of Monsieur Reynardo. It was as though he were the balancing scale between good and evil, and evil and good. Hatred and love, despair and hope played across his features, illuminating them at times like lightning playing behind storm clouds with an unearthly beauty, Satan before the fall.

And to Mouche, who passed in that moment over the last threshold from child to womanhood, there came as a vision of blinding clarity an understanding of a man who had tried to be and live a life of evil, who to mock God and man had perpetrated a monstrous joke by creating his puppets like man, in His image, and filling them with love and kindness.

And in the awful struggle within him that confronted her she read his punishment. He who loved only wickedness and corruption had been corrupted by the good in his own creations. The seven dolls of his real nature had become his master and he their victim. He could live only through them and behind the curtain of his booth.

And in one last blinding flash Mouche knew the catalyst that could save him. It was herself. But he could not ask for her love. He would not and could not ask. In that flash she thought for an instant upon the story of Beauty and the Beast, which had always touched her oddly as a child, and knew that here was the living Beast who must die of the struggle if she did not take pity on him.

Yet it was not pity but love that made Mouche reach her arms toward him across the counter of the puppet booth where they had dueled daily for the past year and cry, "Michel— Michel! Come to me!"

No time seemed to have passed, yet he was out of the booth and they were clinging desperately to one another. Trembling, holding him, Mouche whispered, "Michel . . . Michel. I love you. I do love you, no matter who or what you are. I cannot help myself. It is you I love, you that I have always loved."

It was she who held him secure, his red head, as stiff and bristly as that of Mr. Reynardo, sheltered in the hollow of her neck and shoulder where so often his hand, unrecognized, had leaned. And the desperation of his clinging was the greater as he murmured her name again and again, "Mouche . . . Mouche . . . Mouche . . ." and hid his face from hers.

"Michel . . . I love you. I will never leave you."

Then it was finally that Mouche felt the trickling of something warm over the hand that held the ugly, beautiful, evil but now transfigured head to her and knew that they were the tears of a man who never in his life had yielded to them before and who, emerging from the long nightmare, would be made forever whole by love.

And thus they remained on that darkened empty stage for a long while as Michel Peyrot, alias Capitaine Coq, surrendered his person and his soul to what had been so fiercely hateful and unbearable to him, the cloister of an innocent and loving woman and the receiving and cherishing of love.

Nor did they stir even when an old Negro with a white patch over one eye shuffled across the echoing stage and, looking down over the counter of the booth into the darkness of the mysterious quarters below, chuckled.

"Oh ho, little boss! You, Carrot Top! Mr. Reynardo! Dr. Duclos, Ali, Madame Muscat! Where are you all? You better come up here and learn the news. Miss Mouche is not going to leave us. She going to stay with us forever."